FLIRTING with the ENEMY

AN ENEMIES TO LOVERS ROMANTIC COMEDY

GIA STEVENS

Flirting with the Enemy: An Enemies to Lovers Romantic Comedy by Gia Stevens

www.authorgiastevens.com

Published by: Gia Stevens

Copyright: Flirting with the Enemy: An Enemies to Lovers Romantic Comedy by Gia Stevens © 2022 Gia Stevens

Print Edition: 978-1-958286-07-4

Editor: My Notes In The Margins

v060725

To Grandma
I love you but don't read this book.

(There's lots of naughty words and S.E.X.)

chapter one
Alligator Bow Tie

Parisa

If my life wasn't a steaming pile of dog shit sitting in the scorching hot sun right now, I don't know what else it would be. I can't lose this folder. My entire future at The Blue Stone Group depends on it. Maybe not my entire future, but definitely the foreseeable future.

"Shit. Shit. Shit," I mumble to myself. I frantically shove papers around my desk searching for the manilla file folder I need for this meeting. "Where did I put it?" Maybe it fell behind my desk? Pushing my desk chair back, it glides across the vinyl mat leaving me room to crouch down to my hands and knees and search under my desk. When was the last time someone cleaned under here? My hand swipes cracker crumbs off to the side. Wait. Do they expect me to do it? With my face down, ass up, and still under my desk, a voice from behind causes me to freeze.

"Lose something?" His deep voice sends my hackles to the sky.

And here comes another dog to add to that steaming pile of shit.

I crawl out, backward. While still on my hands and knees, my eyes catch sight of his brown Italian loafers. As my gaze drifts upward, I take in his perfectly ironed gray slacks and his crisp, white shirt that's precisely tucked into his pants. But my perusal pauses on his god-awful navy bowtie. Who still wears bow ties? Then a tan folder catches my attention.

"Yes. That. I need that." I climb to my feet and yank the folder out of his hand, the sudden movement causing me to get a whiff of his cologne. Citrus and cedar. Not overpowering, but a clean fragrance. I flip through the folder to make sure nothing is missing.

"Also, if you didn't see the email, Mr. Evans wants you to print out the last marketing report." Seth checks his watch. "Oh, and the meeting starts in five minutes." A smirk flashes across his face before he turns and meanders through the sea of cubicles on his way to Conference Room B. Both of us are marketing associates at The Blue Stone Group, the largest real estate and development firm in Harbor Highlands. The draw of Lake Superior creates a high demand for real estate in Northern Minnesota.

Dammit. Turning around, I find my mouse and give it a wiggle to wake up my computer. Come on. Hurry up. My fingers fly across the keyboard as I enter my password. I search for the report and press print. I wait. And wait. Nothing. What the hell is wrong? I check the screen on the printer. Load Paper Tray 2 flashes on the LCD. Why does today hate me? I stand up and yank open the overhead cubby door. I grab the ream of paper and fill the stupid tray. Once it's satisfied, it spits out the printed pages and I gather them as each one prints. The stack is still warm in my hands as I make a dash for the conference room. Ugh! The manilla file folder. Quickly, I spin on my heel and take a few steps back to my cubicle and snag it off my desk. I shove the papers into the file folder and haul ass to the other side of the office.

"I'm here. I'm here." I rush through the door and past the row of people already seated. When I find my chair on the opposite side, I take a seat and place my papers on the table. Everyone sits in silence as I get situated and attempt to control my erratic breathing. Maybe I should take Olivia up on those yoga classes.

"Glad you could join us, Ms. Anthony. Did you print off that report for me?"

"Yes. Of Course, I did." My hands fumble with the folder as I retrieve the papers and pass them to Mr. Evans. His salt and pepper hair glimmers as the morning sun shines through the floor to ceiling windows.

He glances over the papers, quickly thumbing through them before placing the stack on the long rectangular table and continuing with the meeting that takes longer than any meeting should. While Mr. Evans rambles, my gaze drifts to *him*. The enemy. Seth Taylor. His perfectly messy styled hair. The black framed glasses that rest on his perfectly shaped nose. In profile, the sun radiates off his smooth, freshly shaven skin. My eyes continue to follow the contours of his face, over his chin, past his lips, the top slightly thinner than the bottom, and then down to his Adam's apple. Are those alligators on his bow tie?

"Parisa. You'll get me that document?" Mr. Evans' question pulls me from my shameless gawking.

"Uh. Yeah. Document. Got it." I hastily stack all the other papers in front of me when I catch sight of Seth, a slight smirk on his face as he shakes his head before rising from his seat. Not wanting to give myself away, I jump up from my chair and square my shoulders as I clutch the now rumpled papers in my grasp. Once Seth is out of the room, my shoulders deflate. Quietly, I finish organizing the papers and when I get back to my desk, I throw the folder next to my keyboard and plop down in my chair.

"Shit. What document did he want from me?" I rest my elbows on my desk and drop my head into my hands.

"He wanted the papers for the upcoming conference." With my cheek still resting on my hand, I turn my face to follow the voice coming from my right over the half wall separating our desks.

"Of course, you would know exactly what he wants."

Without looking up Seth replies, "I pay attention when I'm in meetings. Helps me to know what's happening in the company. You should get yourself a digital calendar or a notes app. It will help you stay organized."

It's not that I'm disorganized. I just consider it organized chaos. I silently mock him with exaggerated facial expressions.

"Yeah. I saw that."

I throw my hands up in the air. "Of course you did," I mumble under my breath.

"And I heard that."

"Do you have extra spidey senses today, or what?" Irritation laces my voice. "And what's this conference?"

This time his head does pop up. His piercing green eyes bore into mine. "It's in the email. You might want to familiarize yourself with it because we're going to be spending even more time together." He goes back to jotting down notes.

Email? What email? I might have to contact IT to let them know I'm not getting my emails because I haven't seen any emails. I log into my computer and open my email. Oh. There it is. I spend the next few minutes reading and rereading the words on the screen.

"This is bullshit," I blurt out.

A small chuckle sounds from my right. "Bullshit it is not."

I drop my head to my desk and slowly bang my forehead against the surface. Maybe if I'm concussed, they'll make someone else go. Because the last thing I want is to spend even more time with Seth.

chapter two
Sweet Victory

Seth

She's not the only one who's overjoyed with this travel arrangement for the conference. I would rather fly in the cargo hold than sit next to her. Okay, that might be a stretch, but why her? When I peer to my left, she's staring at her screen reading the same email I just finished. Her head slowly turns toward me, and I can't help but flash her a bright smile knowing it will drive her crazy. Her gaze bores into mine for a few beats before she huffs, pushes away from her desk, and storms away. I'm stunned. I've never known her to not say anything. Did I finally break her? A moment later, Parisa storms back. Spoke too soon.

She stands at the corner of my desk. "This isn't happening. I'm talking to Mr. Evans. At the very least, I want my seat as far away from yours as possible."

I just smile at her knowing it will infuriate her more.

"Ugh!" She throws her hands in the air and turns around.

My gaze is fixated on her auburn hair that skirts around her. Once again, she's stomping away like a petulant child and, for whatever reason, I have a hard time keeping the smirk off my face. Wait, I know why. I take great pleasure in her annoyance. Then a ding draws my attention back to my computer as I read the subject line.

☐ ☆ The Blue Stone Group Employees   New Position Available: Marketing Director   ▣ 🗑 ✉ ◷

I've been waiting for this day. Several months ago, I caught wind that Cindy, the current marketing director, was retiring soon, and it appears the time is now. Moving the cursor of my mouse over the email, I click and scan the words. Getting this position would mean so much, not only for my career, but the pay raise would come in handy in helping my parents. I move the email to my *Important* folder for later.

My desk phone rings and when I glance over, *Bennett Pierce* flashes on the screen. Someone's having a crisis. If I had to guess, it's Trey. I grab the receiver and hold it up to my ear. "This is Seth."

"Dude, I called you. Of course, I know it's you."

"Just making sure you didn't accidentally dial the wrong number. Like that time you called me instead of the girl in home staging and proceeded to tell me exactly what your tongue was going to do to her that night."

Laughter erupts from the other end. "Shit. Forgot about that. Her extension had the same numbers as yours just flip flopped. But you know I would have offered you the same treatment."

"What you and your tongue were going to do , I didn't

want you doing to me. Hard pass. On that note, what do you want?"

"Come down to my office. Trey's having a crisis."

"He's always in crisis. I'll be down in a moment."

I hang up the phone, rest my elbows on my desk, and thread my fingers through my hair, the marketing director position sitting at the forefront of my mind. I need to think of every possible way to secure that position. Pushing away from my desk, I stand and swivel on my heel, but suddenly my body jolts backward. All I hear is an oomph and papers flutter to the floor. When I lift my gaze, I'm met with a violent storm of hazel glaring back at me.

"Shit. Sorry. Let me help you." I bend to collect the fluttering papers before they hit the floor. I may be a lot of thing but I'm not always a jerk, especially when I'm at fault.

"You know what, don't bother." Parisa bends over at the same time and our heads smack against each other. "Shit" Her hand flies up to her forehead, caressing the spot of impact.

"Sorry." I finish collecting the papers in a pile and pass them to her. "Do you want me to get you a bag of ice?"

"No. It's fine. I'm sure you'd figure out a way to sabotage the ice." She clasps the papers to her chest while still rubbing her forehead.

"It's just ice."

"You'd poke a hole in the bag so all the melted ice would drip on me or something."

"Now that you mention it, let me get you some ice." I cock my head to the side.

Parisa stands to her full height and narrows her eyes at me. "I wouldn't take ice from you if it were the last ice on the planet," she sneers. Then she sidesteps me and stomps back to her cubicle, one hand still rubbing her forehead while the other holds the askew stack of papers.

I knock on Bennett's door before letting myself in. Bennett and Trey are bickering about the baseball game last night. Without interrupting their heated debate, I take a seat in the leather armchair next to Trey. Just as I sit down, two sets of eyes turn their attention to me and the room gets quiet. Then my gaze darts between the two of them before breaking the silence.

"What's up, guys? What's the crisis?"

Trey stands up and fumbles with his belt buckle. "I got this rash—"

Bennett busts out laughing while I punch Trey in the thigh. "Go to a doctor. I'm sure you have more than just a rash. But really, that's why you called me down here?"

Trey rubs his hand over the sore spot, and he sits back down. "We heard about the job opening. You applying?"

"Of course I am. I would be stupid not to. The only problem is Parisa. I know she'll want that position just as much. And I'm slightly terrified she'll try to shank me in the parking garage to get it."

"Ah yes, the damsel not in distress. You'll have some competition. She's a firecracker. You'll have to keep an eye out if you see her whittling a shiv at her desk." Trey crosses his ankle over his knee.

"Perhaps. I can't imagine she knows anything about whittling or shivs. But either way, when I get it, that'll make the victory that much sweeter."

Bennett rests his elbows on his desk. "Say you get it. You think she'll stick around if you're her boss?"

"Not my problem." I lift a shoulder and let it drop. But my dick twitches at the thought of bossing her around.

Well shit. That's new.

chapter three
What Can Go Wrong?

Parisa

When I return to my desk, Seth's gone. I blow out a sigh of relief. No one can infuriate me more than him. Not even the guy who passes me in his car only to cut back into my lane and slows down. I hate that guy. And just thinking of Seth trumps that guy. Everything he does irritates me. Every morning it's the same routine. He'll click his pen and place it vertically next to his perfectly square mouse pad. Then he places his coffee mug directly above that and last but not least, he strategically places his mouse so it's positioned at the best arm angle. Why bother? It's just going to get messed up anyway.

Then I get an idea. I peer over my shoulder to make sure no one's watching. When I see the coast is clear, I stand and round the corner into his cubicle. I slightly rotate his pen holder, move some papers to the other side of his desk, and remove all the staples from his stapler. A brushed silver picture frame perched on the side of his computer screen catches my attention. Without a second thought, I pick it up for a closer inspection. This picture must be from a few years back. Seth looks younger, and he's not wearing a bow tie. I was convinced he was born wearing one. Apparently, I was wrong. He's standing next to an older couple who I assume are his parents from the uncanny resemblance. Next to them is an older guy and a younger girl. Maybe Seth's siblings?

Voices from the other side of the room startle me. My heart rate spikes as I fumble to set the picture frame back down and scurry back to my desk. Just as I whirl my chair back toward my computer, two men stroll past me. When I look up, I flash them a tight smile as they walk by. My gaze lingers on them until they're out of sight. That was a close one.

I wiggle my mouse and the computer screen comes to life. Clicking the mail icon, the email I've been waiting for sits at the very top of the list. Quickly, I read the email then read it a second time. This is exactly what I need for myself and my career. Opportunities like this don't come around very often and I can't let what happened at my last job hinder my chances. My desk phone rings and Olivia Ellis flashes on the screen. Picking up the receiver, I press it to my ear. Before I can get a word out, Olivia is speaking on the other end.

"Lunch time. Come down. We'll get food."

I glance at the time on my computer. No wonder I feel all out of sorts, it's past noon. "I'll be right down." Hanging up, I stare at the email one more time as my lips pull into a smile before I set my computer to sleep.

When I arrive at the first floor, Olivia is already waiting

for me with her purse slung over her shoulder, blonde locks cascading down her back as she talks with Charlie. Both Olivia and Charlie work reception at The Blue Stone Group. Olivia and I have been best friends since we started working here eighteen months ago and Charlie joined our girl gang when she started here almost a year ago.

"You guys won't guess what just happened. I got the email!" I can't fight the excitement in my voice. Both Olivia and Charlie shriek with excitement. "This is just the first step. I need to apply and then get the job. But I've been waiting for this moment."

"No one deserves this position more than you." Olivia pulls me in for a hug.

"So, you'll probably be competing against Seth for the position?" Charlie asks.

My shoulders slump. There goes the wind in my sails. Just hearing his name makes me want to stab myself in the ear with a sharp object. "Yeah. As far as I know. From what I've heard around the office, we're the only two internal candidates interested." The Blue Stone Group has always prided itself on treating their employees fairly and wanting to promote from within. Opposed to my last job, who wouldn't know what fair was even if it smacked them in the face.

After we're done with our lunch, we quickly grab a coffee and walk back to the office. The fall breeze picks up and I tug my cardigan around me. I stop a few steps shy of the front door.

Olivia pauses and turns back to me. "Everything alright?"

"I forgot my phone charger in my car. I'm going to run

up to the parking garage really quick and grab it. I'll chat with you later."

Olivia gives me a wave before heading through the double glass doors. I turn around to enter the parking garage next door. While I ride the elevator up to the third floor, I mindlessly scroll through my social media, not caring about my battery's slow death, since I'll have my charger soon. When the doors open, I toss my phone into my black Kate Spade tote as I stroll to my car. As I approach, I press the key fob to unlock the doors. Crawling onto the driver's seat, I set my coffee in the cup holder and search for my charger, starting with the glove box, no charger. I open the center console, empty. I peer around the seat as I scan the backseat and the floor. Nothing. Shit. Where did it go? A white cord catches my attention on the passenger side floorboard. Stretching across the car, I reach for the cord. I tug, but it won't budge. What the hell is it caught on?

Bending over farther, I use two hands and finally tug it free. If someone were behind me, I'm sure they would get a full view of my ass. Just as I sit up, victorious with the cord in my hand, a blaring car horn echoes off the cement causing me to jump and smack the back of my head against the door frame. *Son of a bitch.* I rub the growing bump on the back of my head and grab my coffee, stepping out onto the cement. Slamming the car door closed, I lock it and throw my keys into my bag while I fish around for my phone. I swear this bag is like a black hole or something. While I continue to dig in my bag, I round the corner of the SUV parked next to me, but I'm immediately jolted back. That's when I feel it. A warm liquid seeps through my white boho style blouse, hitting my cool skin. The plastic coffee lid and charging cord fall to the now wet cement.

"Ah shit. Sorry."

My eyes pinch shut at the sound of his voice. When I slowly open my eyes, Seth is rising to the standing position, his fingers curled around my phone cord.

"Two run-ins in one day. The universe must be conspiring against us." He holds the cord out to me, but as soon as I reach for it, he pulls it back. "Wait, maybe I shouldn't give this back. You'll probably try to strangle me with it."

"The thought has crossed my mind." I lunge for my cord and steal it from his grip like a ninja. At least I'm winning at something today. Then I remember my soaking wet shirt. Seth's gaze follows mine as the brown wet spot clings to my skin. Pinching the fabric, I pull it away from my chest, hoping to avoid anything becoming see through. "Why weren't you watching where you're walking?"

"Well, I could say the same for you." He takes a sip of his coffee, his hard stare on me over the rim of his reusable coffee cup. "Also, if you used something a little more durable than that flimsy plastic lid for your coffee, you wouldn't have spilled it on yourself. Plus, reusable is much better for the environment." He holds up his metal coffee mug and gives it a wiggle. He walks away, but stops and turns. "If you haven't seen the email yet, Mr. Evans wants to chat with us later, so I suggest you get that," he points to my stain, "cleaned up before the meeting. Don't want to look like a slob."

"How do you know that? We've both been away from our desks."

"Email on my phone. I can get more done that way."

"Overachiever," I mumble under my breath.

Seth continues his walk across the parking garage before coming to a halt in front of a midnight blue hybrid SUV.

Of course, this has to happen to me. I stuff my charging cord into my bag, bend down to pick up the plastic lid, and stomp my way past Seth while not so nonchalantly giving him the middle finger. After tossing the lid into the trash, I decide to take the skywalk into The Blue Stone Group. I really need to keep an extra shirt in my desk drawer, but then again, I never expected something like this to happen.

With my keycard pressed to the scanner, the automatic doors open, and I stride through. Once I'm down the skywalk and into the main building, I immediately spot Charlie and Olivia at the desk. Maybe they can help me out with my shirt situation.

"I leave you alone for like five minutes and this happens." Olivia points to my shirt.

"Tell me about it. Damn Seth."

Like Beetlejuice, you say his name and he appears. Seth casually strolls through the door with a smug smirk on his face. I shoot daggers in his direction his entire walk through the atrium until he comes to a stop at the bank of elevators. Once he's inside, my shoulders relax as I exhale a sigh.

"So, I take it he's the one who caused the brown stain?" Olivia rests her hip against the side of the two-tiered reception desk.

"I got my charger from my car, turned the corner, and wham. Seth was just standing there, staring at his phone. My coffee took the brunt of it, which happens to be on my shirt and the rest on the floor of the parking garage."

"I'm sorry Parisa. Seth should give you his shirt." Charlie laughs.

Now I'm curious what Seth would look like underneath his collared shirt and bow tie. "I'm going to rinse this out the best I can before it stains. I guess I'll just wear my cardigan the rest of the day."

A few hours later, I'm seated beside Seth in Mr. Evans' office. He's typing away on his computer while we wait to see why he wants to see us. My gaze drifts to Seth who's sitting straight, shoulders back in his chair, both feet planted firmly on the ground. I wouldn't be surprised if there was a stick shoved up his ass to make him sit so straight. The sound of Mr. Evans' authoritative voice pulls me from my thoughts.

"It's my understanding that both of you are interested in the Marketing Director position." He clasps his hands on top of his desk as he glances between Seth and me.

"Very interested."

"Yes, that is correct, sir," Seth replies at the same time.

"Good. That's what I like to hear. Either of you would make an excellent candidate. But of course, I will still need you both to formally apply." We both nod in understanding. "Now, we have the real estate conference coming up in Aspen, Colorado, where some of the most influential agents and developers from around the country will be in attendance, and I want both of you to attend this year. It will give you a little perspective on what you'll be getting into. Also, as part of the interview process, I want each of you to give a presentation on the new marketing ideas you would bring to the company." Mr. Evans' gaze shifts from Seth to me. "From there, The Blue Stone Group hiring team, along with the team heading the Aspen branch, will determine the best candidate for the position. It's short notice as the conference is in two weeks, but this will also test how well you work under pressure, and I believe both of you will rise to the occasion. If you're up to the challenge, I recommend getting those applications in today and get started on your presentations. I'll email everything we are expecting from you. Then speak to my new assistant, Kimberly, and she will get your travel documents in order."

"Thank you, Mr. Evans. I'll get on this right away." Seth stands and holds out his hand for Mr. Evans to shake. I quickly follow suit.

"Yes. Thank you. I'll get my application in right now." I flash Mr. Evans a bright smile. Shifting toward Seth, my gaze connects with his and I give him the stink eye. Unable to not have the last word, Seth directs his attention back to Mr. Evans.

"I'll get my application turned in today as well." Seth then turns toward me, lips upturned.

"I'm excited about the enthusiasm from the both of you." Mr. Evans stands and escorts us out of his office.

Seth and I walk side by side back to our desks. My pace is much quicker in order to keep up with his longer stride. There's no way I'll let him think he has any upper hand in this situation.

"Glad to see you found a solution to your stained shirt." Seth peers down at me, eyeing my oversized cardigan.

A bead of sweat forms at my hairline and trickles down my temple. There's a reason why I dress in layers, but with this stain, that isn't an option at the moment. I swipe away the moisture. "No thanks to you. Why do they keep this place like a sauna?"

"You could take your sweater off. Oh wait…" Seth chuckles.

I harden my gaze at him. The desire to kick him in the shin is high right now.

Once we reach our cubicles, I pull out my chair and sit down a moment before Seth sits. I'll take my small victory. Immediately, I pull up the online application and begin filling in all the boxes. When I peek a glance at Seth, instead of filling out his application, he's straightening his desk from when I wreaked havoc on it earlier. My lips tug into a small smile. But soon after, I hear the clicking of a keyboard next to me. As soon as I hit submit, I stand. Then I see Seth push away from his desk and stand as well. Wait, he's finished already. I started before him.

"What are you doing?"

"I'm going to give my information to Kimberly." Seth turns on his heel and makes his way toward Kimberly's office on the other side of the large room.

I pick up my stride to catch up with him. "But how did you finish before me?"

"I don't pussyfoot around. I get my job done. Also, I know it was you who moved the things on my desk."

Heat creeps up my neck as I glance down to the floor. *Shit. Deny. Deny. Deny.* "That wasn't me."

"Then why are your cheeks turning pink?" He quirks an eyebrow. Before I can answer, we're at Kimberly's office. Seth rushes to the half closed door, quickly knocking before pushing the door fully open. "I'm here to give you—"

"We are here to give you our information for the travel documents," I interrupt.

"Ah yes. Mr. Evans said you two would stop by. I will just need your driver's licenses. I will get your plane tickets and hotel accommodations booked, and you can stop in at the end of the week to pick that up."

"What is this?" I stare down at my plane ticket. "DEN is Denver, not Aspen. Why are we landing in Denver?

"I'm so sorry." Kimberly looks up at me. "I must have put in the wrong airport code and by the time I realized it there was nothing I could do. All the flights from Denver to Aspen were booked. Don't worry. Mr. Evans advised me that the company will provide a rental car for you and Seth, and you can drive to Aspen. But the good news is we were able to change your outbound flight to fly out of Aspen."

"Well, thank God for that." I look at my plane ticket again and back to Kimberly. "How long of a drive is it from Denver to Aspen?"

"A little under four hours." A deep voice sounds behind me. Why does my soul die a little every time I hear his voice? Turning around, sure enough, Seth is standing there, his gaze following the words on his own plane ticket. I whirl back toward Kimberly.

"Four hours. I have to be stuck in a car with him for four hours?"

"I can't say it's my ideal way to travel, but here we are. Thank you, Kimberly." Seth holds up his travel documents to her before turning around and walking away.

I nod to Kimberly with a snarky smile before I'm on Seth's heel. "You're seriously okay with this?"

"I'm not going to make a show out if it like you are. It's four hours. We'll survive. What can go wrong?"

chapter four
Who Murdered
A Pine Tree?

Seth

Lifting my wrist, I check my watch. Thirty minutes late. If she's not here in the next five minutes, I'm checking my bag and boarding the plane without her. It's the week of the conference and while I'm excited to see what goes on at one of these, I'm also nervous about the interview. I spent all weekend perfecting my marketing campaign and I think the board will have a hard time saying no to my ideas. At least, I hope that's the case.

My foot taps on the tile floor and I check my watch again. Four minutes. Why did Mr. Evans think this was a good idea? She can barely keep it together on a normal day, let alone one where we're on a time crunch. Three minutes.

"I'm here! I'm here!" Parisa barges through the

automatic double glass doors. "Sorry. I thought I had everything packed and then I didn't. I'm not too late, am I?"

"Only thirty-two minutes late. Let's go." I lift my duffle bag on my shoulder and make my way to the ticket counter. The rumble of Parisa's suitcase wheels trail behind us until we're standing at the counter. "We need to check our bags."

"I just need to see your identification," the middle-aged ticket agent says. I pull out my identification and lift my bag onto the scale. Her long nails click away on the keyboard.

"That's all you brought?" Parisa eyes my duffle bag and small carry on.

"I'm an efficient packer."

"Huh." Parisa glances at her full-size suitcase and smaller carry-on and personal item.

"Ma'am, do you have your identification?" The ticket agent's tone is more stern this time.

"Oh. Yeah. Where did I put it?" Parisa digs through her purse, riffling through every pocket and compartment. I give the ticket agent an apologetic smile but secretly pray Parisa's forgotten hers, so she has to catch a later flight.

Parisa stands and checks her back pocket and pulls out her ID. "Here it is." She holds it out to the now annoyed lady and then hoists her bag onto the scale. Luckily, the scale stops at forty-nine point three pounds. I don't think the ticket agent wants to deal with us any longer.

After she tags all our luggage and hoists them on the conveyor belt, we make our way to security. The best thing about this regional airport is that it takes five minutes, give or take, to get through security. Within a few minutes, we're at our gate, one of the four in the airport. I take a seat to wait for boarding while Parisa roams around the small airport and their one open shop. As soon as they call our boarding group, I'm rising to my feet and move to stand in line. Glancing around me, Parisa is nowhere to be seen. Do I need to put her on a leash or something?

Finally, she pops out of the shop with a twenty ounce coffee in one hand and a small bag of crackers in the other. When she strolls up to me, I eye her coffee. "Did you get the largest coffee they had?"

"No. They had one larger, but I decided to execute some self-control." She glances at me, then to the cup before taking a sip of her piping hot coffee.

"I didn't think that was possible."

She narrows her eyes at me and snarls her lip. I give her a bright smile in return. She turns and faces the front of the line. After they scan our boarding passes, we walk down the jetway until we step on the plane and find our seats. Parisa takes the window seat and I take the one right next to her.

Thirty minutes into our flight, a tap on my right shoulder catches my attention. I tug out my ear bud and turn to Parisa.

"I have to pee."

"Can't you hold it? We're almost to Minneapolis. You can pee there."

"I just drank twenty ounces of coffee. What do you think?" She raises an eyebrow.

Grumbling, I unbuckle my seat belt, stand, and move into the aisle so Parisa can move out of her seat. A few minutes later she returns, and once again, I get up to let her in. "Feel better?"

"Much. Thank you." She flashes me a sweet smile.

After we land, our layover is quick. We have forty-five minutes to get from one end of the airport to the other. On our walk we pass a restroom and I stop. "Do you need to go before we get back on the plane?"

"Very funny. I'm fine. Sorry, I don't have the bladder of a camel like you," she sneers.

I can't help but chuckle. This is starting to become the best part of this trip. How much can I rile her up? "Also, you're sitting in the aisle next. I'm not dealing with your incessant need to pee."

"What if I had a health condition? I bet you would feel like a real jerk for making fun of me."

"Do you have a health condition?"

"Well, no…"

"Then I don't feel like a jerk." I cut in front of her so I get on the plane before she does and can take the window seat.

When we land in Denver, we immediately head to baggage claim and then to find the car rental. I fill out all the paperwork and collect the keys. "Alright, we have a four-hour drive. Do you need to use the restroom?" I bend down to eye level as if I'm talking to a toddler.

"I'm fine. No. Wait. I'll be right back." Parisa takes off toward the nearest restroom.

"Why are you squirming in your seat?" My hands grip the steering wheel as I keep my eyes on the road, but every now and then, from the corner of my eye, I catch a glimpse of Parisa wiggling back and forth.

"I have to pee."

"Didn't you go before we left?"

"I did. But coffee tends to go right through me." She holds up her coffee cup, giving it a shake to prove it's empty. Before we made it out of the car rental, Parisa grabbed another coffee, and I knew this was going to happen. Again.

This time I take my eyes off the road and narrow my gaze at her. All she can offer me is a meek smile. Reaching forward, I tap the screen on the GPS to see where the nearest gas station is located. Luckily, there's one a few miles up the road. "Can you manage to hold it for five more minutes?" Irritation laces my voice. I just want to arrive at the hotel and get out of this confined car with her.

"I'm not a child. And yes, I can wait." Crossing her arms over her chest, she shifts her body toward the door. A few seconds later, she's crossing her legs as well.

I spend the next few minutes in blissful silence. I wish the whole trip was like this. When the gas station sign comes into view, Parisa perks up. As I pull into the parking lot and into a spot by the front entrance, she's throwing the car door open before I shift into park. I turn the ignition off, unsure of how long she's going to take. Surprisingly, she returns quickly, but with another beverage in her hand. I eye the clear bottle, then look up at her.

"It's just water. I promise I won't have to pee in an hour."

I turn over the ignition. "Well, if you do, I hope you have good aim because you'll be using that." I point at the bottle.

"Rude much." She huffs and turns her body to face the door while digging around in her bag until she pulls out her AirPods. When the GPS springs back to life and maps our route again, I flip on the blinker to drive west.

After an hour on the road, the sun dips below the mountain tops as snowflakes flutter from the sky and accumulate on the roadway. As soon as we got off the main road, civilization becomes more and more scarce.

The twisting roads surrounded by pine trees makes it feel like we're in the middle of nowhere.

Parisa plucks out an ear bud and turns toward me. "Why are we not on the highway anymore?"

"I don't know. I've been following the GPS and this is the way it told me to go." My grip on the steering wheel tightens.

"I'm pretty sure it was supposed to be a straight shot from the highway." She taps away on the screen of her phone and holds it out to prove that I'm wrong.

"Do you want me to pull over so you can drive?" I raise an eyebrow at her.

"No," she mumbles under her breath. "If we stay on this road, we should be able to get back on the highway in about twenty miles or so." Parisa leans back in her seat and stares out the window, silence once again taking over the small space. Sadly, it doesn't last long. She sits up straighter in her seat. "The snow is really coming down now. It's getting hard to see."

Every now and then an oncoming car will pass us. With the snow that's falling, along with the snow kicked up from their rear tires, it makes it damn near blizzard conditions. The headlight beams shine on the snowflakes and almost make it feel like you're traveling through hyperspace.

"What do you have the temp set to in here? Hell?" She leans forward and adjusts the temperature controls.

Her sudden movements pull me from my space travel thoughts. I watch from the side as she tears off her jacket, then pulls her hoodie over her head. The glow from the center console provides me with just enough light to see her soft, creamy skin as the hem of her shirt inches upward with the hoodie. Her fingers wrap around the fabric and tug it back down.

"Seth. Slow down. Seth!"

Parisa's scream snaps my attention back to the windshield. At that exact moment, a car rounds the corner, kicking up a trail of snow. For a split second, I can't see anything. And that is all it takes. My foot slams on the brake pedal, but it's too late. The tires lock up, the snow-covered road offering zero traction. The back end slides and I turn the wheel, spinning the car and eventually careening us into the ditch. A blanket of snow flies over the hood and lands on the windshield before coming to a halt. My adrenaline spikes, as my heart feels like it's going to beat out of my chest. I inhale a few deep breaths before turning my head toward Parisa. Her hand splayed across the dash, her chest heaving.

"Are you alright?"

She nods before she answers, her voice soft. "Yes. Are you?"

"Yeah." I peer over at her.

"Asshole." Her eyes fixated on the snow covered windshield.

"That guy was an asshole. He was driving way too fast around that corner and—"

"No. You," Parisa sneers, directing her anger toward me.

"Me? What did I do? I was just driving along and then you started screaming at me." I throw my hands up in the air.

"So, this is my fault? You can't drive and it's my fault?"

With my hands back to gripping the steering wheel, I take another deep breath. "Listen, us arguing won't get us out of this situation any faster. Maybe we can push our way out." I grab the door handle and push, but instantly I'm greeted with resistance. I continue to push the snow with the door until I have enough room to squeeze out, but as soon as my foot hits the snow, I immediately sink into the fresh powder. "Shit, that's not good," I mumble.

"What? What's not good?" Panic wraps around Parisa's words.

"I don't think we're pushing this out ourselves. We'll have to call for a tow." I bring my snow-covered leg back into the car and brush it off as she digs for her phone.

"I don't have service." She holds her phone up, pointing it in every direction as if she'll magically find service.

I grab my phone from my pocket. "Me either. I wonder if the storm took out a tower."

"We're going to die. Freeze to death. Not to mention mountain lions. I bet we'd make the perfect bite size snack." She squeezes her eyes shut as her breaths become quicker.

"We aren't going to die. Everything will be fine. Just take a deep breath. In through the nose. Out through the mouth." She takes my instruction. It only takes a life and death situation for this girl to listen to me. "We saw one car. Surely, we'll see another." Parisa continues her breathing as she nods at me. "I'm going to make sure the tailpipe isn't buried in the snow so we can keep the car running for heat."

The door is easier to open this time as I get out and trudge through the snow to check if the back end is clear. While I'm out here I look around. Nothing but trees and darkness. White flakes continue to fall as I look up at the inky sky. Shit. Maybe we will die out here.

"How does it look?" Parisa yells from the rolled down window.

"Back end is clear. Just keep the car running for now." Parisa rolls the window back up as I lean against the car, trying to think of how we can get out of this mess. After a few minutes, headlights shine through the trees, growing brighter as they near. I climb my way up the steep embankment in hopes I don't miss this passing vehicle. When I reach the top, a truck zooms past blinding me with their headlights as a cloud of snow flutters down on me. Frantically, I wave my hands hoping the person sees me. Red taillights illuminate the dark road as the truck comes to a stop and reverses back. A rusty white Chevy pickup truck stops in front of me. The guy inside leans across the bench seat to crank the side window down.

"What the hell are you doing out here?" He turns on the dome light. A scruffy faced, middle-aged man wearing a flannel jacket and bomber hat comes into view. His raspy voice mimics the rattling of his truck.

"Thanks for stopping. We went in the ditch and need to call a tow truck. Would you be able to help us out?"

"Look kid, if you haven't noticed it's snowpocolypse out here. No tow trucks are coming out in this weather. Everything's shut down until it passes."

"Dammit." I look back toward the car and then back at him.

"There's a motel just up the road. I can bring you there until this storm passes and then you can get a tow," he offers.

"Shit. Y-yeah. Okay. Let me get my friend in the car." I trudge through the snow, following in my previous footsteps to make it a little easier. Parisa is going to kill me. I don't know which would be worse, getting eaten by a mountain lion or facing her wrath when I tell her we're going to a motel in a stranger's truck.

Her gaze shoots to mine the moment I open the car door and poke my head in. "Well, good news, bad news."

"Bad news first, always." She gives me a hopeful look.

"There's a winter storm and no tow trucks."

"And what's the good news?"

"There's a nice gentleman who's offered to give us a lift to a motel up the road until the storm passes." I flash her a cheeky grin in hopes she doesn't strangle me. Her silence has me slowly easing away from the car door, but then her soft voice causes me to pause.

"Okay. Motel until tomorrow and then we can get back on the road." She pulls her sweatshirt over her head and shoves her arms into the sleeves of her coat before zipping it up.

"I'll grab our bags and let him know we'll take the ride." I'm surprised. She's taking this better than I expected. I shut the car door behind me as I round the rear to pop the trunk. I hoist my duffel back over my shoulder as I lift her rolling suitcase out. As I climb back out to the road, I yell for her to grab the car keys and lock up. Just as I finish tossing our bags into the back, Parisa is hunched over, taking her last few steps up the hill.

"What is that?" She points to the offending object in front of her as a piece of rust rattles off the wheel well and drops to the ground.

"That's our ride to the motel, our only ride, and this kind gentleman has graciously offered it to us." I open the door, motioning for her to get in. She peers inside before swinging her gaze back toward me, a stern look on her face.

"You can't be serious?"

"Come on sweetheart, the snow isn't letting up anytime soon," the gruff guy bellows from the other side of the cab.

"Yeah, sweetheart. Better listen to the guy." I flash her a smirk. She narrows her eyes at me before begrudgingly climbing into the truck and I follow behind. "Any idea when the snow is supposed to stop?" I ask.

"Maybe a couple of days. Up here in the mountains you never really know until it stops."

"A couple days? We're going to miss the beginning of the conference," Parisa screeches.

"I'm sure they'll understand. It's not our fault we got caught in a snowstorm," I reassure her.

"Where you two headed?"

"Aspen. We would have been there already if we didn't have to rent a car from Denver." Parisa huffs as she crosses her arms over her chest.

Gruff guy leans over to look at me. "She's a feisty one."

A small laugh escapes me. "She's something alright."

"Hey, I'm right here." She darts her glare between the two of us.

"We know, sweetheart," gruff guy murmurs as he taps the steering wheel.

Within a few minutes, we're pulling into an empty motel parking lot. The red neon vacancy sign shines brightly against the black backdrop while a single light post shines dimly on the blanket of snow covering the ground.

"Thanks so much for the ride. We really appreciate it," I say.

"No problem. Here's the number for a tow truck. They'll help you out once the snow clears." He reaches up to the visor to a clipped stacked of papers and passes me a business card.

The truck comes to a chugging stop near the front door. Parisa's shoving me to open the door before the truck is even in park. Hopping out, I grab our bags from the back and place Parisa's on the ground while throwing my bag strap over my shoulder and following her steps toward the front door. When I'm standing beside her, she turns toward me.

"Where's my suitcase?"

"Back there." I hike my thumb behind me.

"You didn't grab my bag?"

"Nope."

She blows out a huff and stomps her way back to the parking lot to retrieve her suitcase. I watch as she pulls it with two hands since the wheels are useless through the thick snow. Once she reaches me again, she stops and drops the handle.

"If I get murdered here, know that I will make it my mission to haunt you until your last breath."

"I know this isn't the Hilton, but it'll have to do. It's either this or sleep in the car."

"I'm kind of liking my chances with the car."

I twist the knob, push open the door, and we both just stare. To call this place luxurious would be a severe understatement. The main office is outdated with cheap wood paneling on the walls and dingy, worn carpet on the floor. My nose scrunches as soon as the overpowering stench of pine needles hits me.

"What's that smell?" Parisa covers her nose with her forearms. "It's like someone murdered a pine tree in here."

I walk in first and Parisa trails behind me. To the left of the entrance is a reception desk, but there isn't a soul insight. I stroll the the counter and tap the bell and wait. My gaze wanders around the room as Parisa does the same.

"I think I found the stink." I point to a cluster of opened pine tree air fresheners dangling from a thumbtack on the wall.

"Isn't this place… charming." She wrinkles her nose.

An older woman in her sixties with thinning shoulder length gray hair pops out of nowhere, startling us both. "Why thanks, dear. My husband and I have owned this place for over fifty years."

"It's probably been that long since you've last updated it too," she mumbles under her breath.

"Where are my manners? Welcome to The Pine Needle Motel." The old lady flashes us a toothy smile. "How can I help you?"

"We need a room. Our car went in the ditch just down the road and we need to wait out the storm until a tow truck can come help us." I rest an elbow on the desk while Parisa fiddles with a candy dish and other trinkets sitting on the worn wood top.

"Oh my, it's quite the storm out there. We haven't seen a storm like this in September since 1971. We got almost twenty inches of snow over two days."

"Twenty inches?" Parisa's eyes widen in shock. "We're never going to get out of here."

"It's not too often we get these types of storms. But when it's the perfect mix of a low pressure coming from the southwest and a strong Arctic cold front coming from Canada, they collide over the Rocky Mountains and the combination wreaks havoc on everything."

"Yeah. I'm about to do the same thing," Parisa turns around and mumbles.

"We've had a long day. Can you see if you have any rooms?"

Parisa gives me a *well duh* look and I shrug.

"Let me see what I have." She flips open an actual reservation book and thumbs through the pages as if she doesn't know this place is a ghost town.

Parisa leans over the desk to get a view of the reservation book. "This better not be like a cliché romance story where you tell us there's only one room available with only one bed and we have to share. Because if I have to share a room with *him*, I might just kill him."

"Well, dear. It just so happens to look like—" the lady

flips a few more pages in her book, squinting her eyes. *Is she actually reading anything?* Parisa rolls her eyes at her. "It looks like we have two rooms available. Six and seven.

Parisa's shoulders drop in relief. "Great. We'll take them."

After we finish paying for our rooms, we head back out into the snowy night with our room keys in hand. Real metal keys and not the plastic ones. We walk down the snow-covered sidewalk. The only available light becomes dimmer with each step. I watch as each number on the wood doors increase. One. Two. Three. Four. Five. Security Room.

"Why does this place need a security room? I can't imagine they get a lot of visitors out here that would warrant the need for security." She cranks her head back and eyes the door as we pass.

"I don't know, but here's your room. Number six and I'm the next one down." We stand at our respective doors. Just as I have mine open, I see her struggling with hers. "Well, good night, sweetheart. Sleep tight. Don't let the bed bugs bite."

Before I close the door, I hear her mumble, "Oh my God, there better not be bed bugs." Then I hear her cursing her door for not opening and a few seconds later it slams shut.

chapter five
Gray Sweatpants Fantasy

Parisa

I flip on the switch and the lights flicker to life, illuminating the room. When my eyes adjust to the light, I peer around the room. It's quite possible the 1970s threw up all over the floor and walls. The yellow and brown square patterned curtains do nothing to help the feng shui in the room. There's a desk on the opposite wall of the queen size bed with a mirror hanging above it. Along the back is a small open closet and bathroom. The only plus side, the room is larger than I was expecting.

Before getting too comfortable, I scope out the rest of the room. As I enter the bathroom, I click on the switch and a blinding fluorescent light over the mirror strobes to life, followed by a low hum. Definitely outdated, but functional.

Walking back to the main area I stop in front of the bed. The geometric brown patterned quilt is not creating a warm and cozy sleeping atmosphere. I rip back the covers to inspect that there are indeed no bed bugs. Exhaustion takes over as I release a yawn. The sooner I get to bed the sooner this day can be over. Unzipping my suitcase, I riffle through all my clothes before finding my pajamas. Once in hand, I make my way to the bathroom to change and wash my face. When I'm done, I turn on the lamp next to the bed and shut off all the other lights before crawling into bed. Then it dawns on me. My gaze darts to the mirror above the desk. On the other side of that wall is the security room. I spring out of bed, close my suitcase, and hoist it up onto the desktop covering the mirror. Feeling a little triumphant, I crawl back into bed and turn off the lamp.

Unable to get comfortable, I spend the next several minutes tossing and turning. When I'm somewhat satisfied, a loud bang causes my eyes to shoot open, followed by a scratching noise like a fork on a plate. The entire room is dark except for a sliver of light shining in through a crack in the curtain. I hold my breath, hoping to hear the sound again, but all I can hear is the drumming of my heart in my chest. Tiny pricks crawl up my bare arm. Without a second thought, I brush it off. Wait, was that a spider? I scurry off the bed in the opposite direction I brushed the spider and find the nearest light to turn on. Sure enough, a little, black body with eight legs is crawling across the white sheet. A shudder wracks my body as I do everything to tamp down my scream. With eyes still on the spider, I shimmy my way across the room, trying to avoid any sudden movements in case it tries to attack.

Once I'm close to the desk, I hear it. A clicking sound. And that's my cue to get the hell out of here. I shove my feet into my untied boots, throw my jacket over me, and rip open the door. Within seconds, I'm beating my fist on Seth's. Finally, after what feels like forever, he opens the door, wearing only a pair of gray sweatpants that hang dangerously low on his hips. My heart rate accelerates and I'm pretty sure it's not because I just ran out of bed. So, this is what he hides under his bow ties and black rimmed glasses. When my gaze meets his, a sly smirk graces his lips.

"Why aren't you wearing a shirt?" Suddenly distracted by what's in front of me, the question tumbles out of my mouth before I can stop it.

With his forearm resting on the doorframe, he asks, "Why are you at my door?"

"Guys who wear bow ties aren't supposed to have bodies like… that." I motion to his naked chest. "You've definitely ruined my gray sweatpants fantasy." My gaze instinctively wanders back down his chest.

"By the way you can't stop staring, I don't think I've ruined anything."

My head shoots up from where I was admiring—I mean studying—fine, drooling over his bare chest. He's not overly bulky but has some nice definition. "Get to the point," I mutter to myself. I tug my jacket tighter around me. "Switch rooms with me."

"Why?"

"There is a giant spider in my room and it's going to eat me once I fall asleep," I rush out in a single breath.

"What makes you think I want to be eaten?"

I cross my arms over my chest. "What's with all the questions? Just switch rooms with me." I offer him my biggest, saddest puppy dog look.

"So, you have an irrational fear of spiders?"

"I have a perfectly normal fear of anything with more than four legs."

"Ask nicely."

I huff and link my fingers together in front of me. "Pretty please switch rooms with me."

He ponders my plea for a moment. "Nope."

"Ugh! You're so infuriating." I cross my arms.

"How about this?" He drops his arm from the doorframe and twists his body to point toward the corner of the room, taking pity on me. "I have this very uncomfortable chair sitting over in the corner. It's all yours if you want."

I eye the chair, then images of the big, hairy spider flood my mind. Narrowing my gaze at him. "Fine. But please put a shirt on."

He steps out of the way to let me into his room. Immediately, my gaze darts around the space. Of course, he would hang up his clothes, have his shoes lined up by the door, and have everything neat and tidy. My feet carry me over to the chair and I plop down, which was a bad idea because this chair sucks. I rub the underside of my thigh. That's going to bruise tomorrow.

Seth closes the door, strolls to the other side of the room, and pulls a t-shirt off a hanger. He shoves his arms through the sleeves before tugging it over his head. I can't help but watch as his back muscles flex and shift with each movement. When he turns around, I quickly divert my gaze, praying he hasn't caught me gawking at him once again. He crawls into bed and leans against the headboard. He reaches for a book turned over on the nightstand and continues to read. Obviously, he has the body of a God and reads. I'm starting to think the universe hates me. But then an idea pops into my head.

"Seth? Can you do me a favor?" I ask in the softest, sweetest voice I can muster.

His eyes peer at me over the top of his book as he quirks an eyebrow without saying anything.

"Can you get my suitcase from my room?" I flash him a charming smile, but I can tell he's annoyed. Seth releases a loud exhale before setting his book back down and climbing out of bed. He throws on his jacket and shoves his feet into his shoes.

"Thank you!" I thrust the key at him before he can say no. As soon as the door shuts behind him, I beeline it for his warm spot on the bed. I am not sleeping on that godforsaken chair. He can sleep on the chair. Was it a dirty move? Absolutely. Do I regret it? Not for one second.

A few minutes later, Seth is strolling through the door with my suitcase in tow. He rolls the bag into the room, removes his jacket, and turns his gaze on me while I lie in his bed.

"What are you doing?"

"Going to sleep." I wiggle my butt, pretending to get cozy.

"I don't think so. You can sleep over there." He points to the chair.

"Nope."

Seth narrows his gaze. "You know what? Fine. I get it." Seth saunters toward the bed and rests his hands on the comforter, bending down so his face is in front of mine. His breath is a whisper across my skin. "You just want to sleep with me. It's okay. Your secret's out, *sweetheart.*" He emphasizes the last word.

"You wish. I just happen to hate spiders more than I hate you. And let me say, I really hate spiders." My jaw clenches. He rounds the bed and pulls back the covers before crawling in and tugging the blanket up to his waist as he lies on his back. I turn off the lamp, shrouding the room in darkness. Shimmying down, I lie next to him, but then my eyes dart toward the door. After a few minutes, I break the silence. "Seth?" He answers with a grumble. "Can you switch sides with me?"

"You've got to be kidding me. Why?"

I roll over to face him. "Well, this side is closest to the door and if someone breaks in, I'm going to be the first one they encounter and, most likely, the first one they murder."

"And why do you think I want to be the first one murdered?"

"Please, this is the last favor. I promise."

"I highly doubt that," he says under his breath. Seth rips the blanket off him before rounding the bed to switch spots as I scoot over to the other side. After finally feeling settled, I'm just about to drift off when Seth's voice cuts through the silence.

"Parisa?"

"Yeah?"

"Why was your suitcase on the desk?"

"Oh, that." I let out a small chuckle. "When we were walking to our rooms earlier, I noticed there's a security room next to mine, which seemed odd. When I got in my room, I realized the desk and mirror share a wall with the security room and I've watched a lot of *Dateline*. Something told me it was a two-way mirror and some creeper was on the other side recording me. Then there were some clicking sounds like an old recorder."

"Sorry I asked." Seth tugs the blanket up and rolls on to his side, his back facing me. I do the same. I can't believe I'm sharing a bed with Seth. The bow tie wearing neat freak with a chest I want to run my tongue across. I mentally scold myself. What am I thinking? I don't like him. My body just naturally reacts to another attractive person and that's it. I. Do. Not. Want. Him.

chapter six

It Started With A Kiss

Seth

The morning light shines in through a gap in the curtain, stirring me awake. Oddly enough, that was the best sleep I've gotten in a while. Must have been the exhaustion from everything that happened yesterday. Last night, before Parisa came to my room there was still no cell service, so I went to the front desk to call Mr. Evans to notify him that a snowstorm stranded us somewhere between Denver and Aspen. Apparently, they got hit with the same storm. I'll have to see what the weather is like today and hopefully we can get out of here.

When I move to sit up, something heavy is draped across my chest. Slowly, I peer down. All I see is a mess of auburn locks and instantly my body stiffens. It slipped my mind that Parisa came to my room and slept in my bed last night. My gaze flits over her cheekbone and down her sloping nose that has a slight upturn at the end. Her full, pouty lips slightly parted as she breathes softly. Slender fingers splayed out across my chest. My dick twitches at the thought of her in my bed with me. Wait. Not *her* per se, but the thought of a warm body next to me. That must be it. Either way, if she wakes up and finds me with a semi, who knows what she'll do? I know one thing, though. I don't want to find out.

Her eyes flutter open as if she knew I was thinking about her. Her fingers lightly trail along my chest. Once she realizes who she's cuddled next to, she scurries away. I pretend to be asleep to save her the embarrassment, but I really miss her warmth. When I feel the other side of the bed dip down, I fake a yawn and stretch so she knows I'm awake.

"Did you sleep well?"

"Uh y-yeah. Really good, actually. What time is it?" She turns to look at me over her shoulder.

For a brief moment, I catch her gaze drift over the sliver of bare skin where my shirt has ridden up before she turns her head back around, but it's too late. I've already caught her. I check my phone on the nightstand. "Looks to be shortly after eight a.m."

She nods before standing up and making her way to the bathroom. I hear the running water splashing against the porcelain sink through the closed door. A few minutes later she returns to the common area, this time her hair in one of those messy buns plopped on the top of her head.

"I'm going to see what the weather looks like." She tugs on her boots and wraps her coat around her, and then she's out the door.

As soon as she's out of sight, I bolt out of bed and head to the bathroom. Get your shit together. She's just a girl who slept in your bed. But God, it felt good to have a body pressed up against mine. It's been way too long. But let's not forget she hates you with every fiber of her being. Unfortunately, my dick didn't get the memo and wants to go back to cuddling. I turn the shower on. Steam fills the small area as images of Parisa lying on the bed, her auburn hair fanned out over the pillows as I hover over her, flash through my mind. I wonder how fast I can rub one out? Tearing back the shower curtain, I step inside, the hot water spraying over my overheated skin. Rivers of water run down my chest as I grab my dick at the base, making quick strokes at first. I rest my other hand against the shower wall in front of me. My head bows as I pick up the pace of my strokes.

Fuck. One night in bed with this girl and she already has me in knots. But I can't stop thinking about her. Again, I chastise myself. It can't be her. Just the idea of her. I can imagine it's any gorgeous woman and I'll get the same results. Images of models, actresses, the pretty barista from the coffee shop down the street from The Blue Stone Group flash through my thoughts. But nothing. When my mind drifts back to the auburn-haired bombshell snuggled up to me this morning, my dick jolts back to life. With each pass, my grip becomes longer and harder. My breathes grow shallow with each stroke. When I reach the tip I squeeze. Images of Parisa on her knees flash before me. I paint her plump, pink lips with the head of my dick before shoving it to her waiting mouth. I grunt as my grip around my shaft grows tighter. Suddenly, my balls tighten up as I feel the impending release. My toes curl against the porcelain covered cast iron tub as a euphoric rush invades my body. I continue to pump my fist until spurts of cum paint the shower wall. Damn. It's been a while since I've had an orgasm like that.

Just as I turn the shower knob to off, I hear the front door close. With my pent-up frustration washed down the drain, I can think straight again. I wonder if she's having the same thoughts as me? Deciding I want to have a little fun with her, I wrap a towel around my waist and stroll out to the room.

Bent at the waist, her firm round ass is in the air as she digs through her suitcase. I take a moment to enjoy the view until I clear my throat. Her back shoots ramrod straight before turning around with her phone charger in hand. Once she takes in the sight in front of her, she loses her grip on the charger and it drops to the floor. A dusty rose color covers her cheeks as she realizes I'm wearing nothing but a towel wrapped around my waist and once again she's staring.

"Oh, sorry." She gives her head a shake and bends down to collect her charger from the ground. "Phone's dead. Gotta charge it." She holds up the charger. "Also, they had coffee and some granola bars and travel cereal bowls with milk. I didn't know what you wanted so I just grabbed a bunch of things." She holds out a coffee, looking anywhere but at me.

"Thanks." I grab the cup from her hand. Our fingers touch and just the slightest caress of her skin on mine makes my dick jump. I don't know if I'll be able to survive another night with this girl.

"Also, the snow is still coming down pretty good. The lady at the front desk said it should pass by tomorrow, so unfortunately, we're stuck here for another night. But there is a vending machine full of delightful snacks and ramen cups to keep us warm." She gives me a playful smirk.

"Well, doesn't that all just sound… appetizing. I guess I'll get dressed to sit around the room all day."

With my back against the headboard, I read through the paperwork my parents gave me with all the information about their non-profit, which includes their business plan, along with future projects. They wanted a second pair of eyes to make sure everything looked presentable. They got a partial grant to fund a new building, but it might be a struggle to secure the rest from the bank. If I get this promotion, I can give them my extra income, then they won't have to worry about the bank.

"I'm so bored." Parisa throws her e-reader on the bed next to me.

I pry my eyes from the folder of papers and glance at her. "You do realize it's only been like two hours. We still have the whole day ahead of us."

"I know. And when your favorite book can't even hold your attention, something's wrong."

"What's your favorite book?" I nod to her e-reader that's sitting screen down on the bed.

"*Dear Life* by Meghan Quinn. It's romance. It's about four people who deal with love and loss. It's a little emotional for me right now. Maybe I should find something smutty." The room is silent for a moment. "What are you reading?"

"Not anything smutty."

She playfully smacks my arm and laughs. "Well, obviously."

"It's just paperwork."

"But what's it for?"

"My parents run a non-profit, The Lilith House, that supports the less fortunate in the community. They're in the process of finding a new building so they can provide more services and help more people."

Parisa sits up and crosses her legs. "Oh, wow, that's amazing. I've heard of that place. It's like a community kitchen, right?"

I set my papers down on the nightstand. "That's just a part of it. They also provide clothing and other basic necessities. They help people find housing and employment. The building they have now is old and outdated. The upkeep is starting to cost more than it's worth. With a new building, they can get better equipment for the kitchen and have more space overall."

"Do you help them run that?"

"I volunteer in the kitchen every week. That's one thing my parents instilled in us growing up. Help those who are less fortunate."

"Who's us?"

"Me, my older brother, and younger sister."

"That's really amazing that you help out. Sorry to have disturbed you. I'll let you get back to it." She turns away to lean against the headboard.

"That's okay. I was beginning to go cross-eyed from all the legal jargon."

"Want to play a game, then?" She claps her hands in front of her in excitement.

"We're kinda limited with what we got here."

"I got it." She jumps off the bed and strolls over to her bag, pulling out a notebook and holding up a couple of pens. "So, it'll be like twenty questions. We'll both write get-to-know-you questions and put them in a pile. One at a time, we'll draw a question, and you have to answer. You can be as incriminating as you want, but just know you might get your own question." A devilish smile forms on her lips.

"Any question?" I sit up and grab a pen from her.

"Any question your heart desires."

We spend the next several minutes writing questions down and folding them up to put in a pile in the middle of the bed. Once we've used up all our paper, we get comfortable. I lay down on my side and prop my head up with my hand as Parisa sits cross legged across from me, the pile of papers between us.

"Well, ladies first." I motion my hand over the folded pieces of paper.

She inspects the pile for a second before reaching in to grab a piece. While her fingers peel back the layers of paper, she gazes up at me through her lashes. A small smile plays on her lips. Excitement and intrigue dances in her hazel irises. Once the paper is unfolded, she scans the words before crumbling it up and throwing it on the bed with a huff.

"What's the question?" I ask, amused at her reaction.

She rolls her eyes. "What's your favorite color? That's a lame question."

"Well, you have to answer it. Those are *your* rules."

"It's green. My favorite color is green. Your turn." She points to the pile.

I release a small laugh and pluck out a piece of paper, reading it out loud. "What's your favorite movie?"

"These questions are bullshit." Parisa rips it from my hands to make sure that's the actual question, then crumples it and tosses it with the other one. "Go ahead and answer."

I ponder the question as if I'm on *Who Wants To Be A Millionaire*. Running through all the possible choices, but there's only one choice. "*Back to the Future*. First is the best. Second one is okay but the third one was terrible. Your turn."

"You took way too long to answer that." She reaches

in, grabs a piece of paper, and unfolds it. Her eyes go wide as she clutches the piece of paper to her chest.

"Remember, it's your game. You gotta answer."

She pulls the paper back so she can read it. "Where's the riskiest place you've had sex?"

Instinctively, I lean in a little closer, anticipating her answer. I imagine this girl has a wild side because she has been nothing but feisty toward me.

After a few long seconds, she bites her bottom lip and closes her eyes as she quickly lets it out. "The bathroom of a fast-food restaurant."

"Oh, someone wanted more than fries with that." I give her a teasing smirk.

She leans over and smacks my forearm. "I was in my twenties and sometimes you can't help when you get the urge."

"So, the milkshake *really does* bring all the boys to the yard."

We both fall into a fit of laughter. We continue with the back and forth of questions and answers for several more rounds. Some questions are very general, but a couple are more risqué. I reach in, grab a piece of paper, and I read the words to myself.

"Come on. You need to read it out loud."

Shit. Do I lie? Tell her the truth? I've never been a liar, so here goes nothing. "When was the last time you masturbated?"

"Oh, that's a good one. So, Seth, when was the last time you did the sausage handshake?" She waggles her eyebrows.

Looking her straight in her eyes I ask, "Really? Is that what you call it?"

"Stop stalling and answer the question."

"This morning," I deadpan.

The smile falls from her lips and the color drains from her face. She leans in a whispers, "Wait, did you masturbate while I was sleeping?"

When I don't answer right away, she grabs the pillow and throws it at me, smacking me in the chest. "Seth! That's creepy!"

I pick up the pillow and throw it back at her. "You weren't in the room. It was when you got coffee and I took a shower." I don't mention I was thinking about her the entire time. So, I divert the question back to her. "When was the last time you did a little finger painting?"

"Finger painting? What the hell is that?"

"Oh, you know." I hold up two fingers like I'm fingering the air.

"That's a terrible name. And it wasn't my question, so I don't have to answer."

"Maybe we should throw that one back in there, then." I reach for the paper, but she slaps my hand away.

"Not so fast. That's not how the game goes." She scolds me, but the gleam in her eyes tells me something else.

"I'm starting to think you're making up the rules as we go." This time I get a full belly laugh as she falls over onto the bedspread. She has never looked so adorable. In fact, I don't think I've ever seen her like this. She seems so alive and carefree. And most importantly, doesn't seem to hate me as much and that thought puts a smile on my face.

Finally, when she collects herself, she brushes a lock of hair out of her face before tilting her head to the side. "Why are you looking at me like that?"

"Like what?" I ask, knowing she knows exactly what I'm thinking.

"Like you either want to kiss me, or you've just figured out your plan on how to kill me and hide my body."

I sit up and lean over so I'm right in front of her. "Well, it's definitely not the second one."

Her eyes search mine intently, waiting for me to make the next move. The air between us crackles with tension. Her breathing becomes heavier as her lips part slightly. I know she wants me to kiss her, but not yet. I need her to want this as badly as I do. Slowly, I back out of her space and throw myself on the bed, my back resting on top of the blanket. "I like this side of you, that's all. You're fun and carefree."

"Just trying to make the best out of a shit situation, I guess. I never imagined I would be here with you, but you're turning out to be *not* horrible company."

"That's a compliment coming from you."

She flashes me a bright smile as she grabs another piece of paper and reads the question. "What makes you smile?" Her eyes flit toward the ceiling while she tries to find the perfect answer. "The sun shining after a thunderstorm." She nonchalantly discards the paper onto the pile with the rest of already asked questions.

"Why's that?"

She ponders her answer for a moment. "The sun is something warm and bright, so when it comes out after a storm, it seems to take away all the bad and replace it with something good and it's comforting."

"Never thought of it that way, but I like it." I reach over and grab a piece of paper. Unfolding it, I read it to myself, but not liking the question, I decide to take this game in a new direction. I look down at the words scribbled in pen then look up into her hazel eyes meeting my green. "Kiss the other person in the room."

chapter seven

You're A Cuddler?

Parisa

I'm stunned. Is that what's written on the paper? Because I didn't write that, so he must have. But he wouldn't write that. Why would he write that?

"You're such a liar. It doesn't say that." I stretch my arm to grab the paper from him, but he's faster.

"You didn't have to write kiss me on a piece of paper to kiss me. You could have just done it." His eyes crinkle in the corners as he continues to hold the piece of paper away from me.

I have to admit after seeing him shirtless last night, waking up snuggled against his chest, and then seeing him in just a towel this morning, I did want to kiss him. But I chalked that up to this dry spell and it could have been any guy, not just Seth. Clearly, my vagina doesn't know the difference.

"I didn't write that. You must have." A smile tugs at my lips. This time I pounce on him to get closer to the paper. But he's still faster. I swing my leg over his hips so I'm straddling his waist as I continue reaching for his hand. I use my knee to pin one of his wrists as my body squirms on top of his. Both of us laugh at the ridiculousness happening right now. Suddenly, in one swoop, I'm flipped onto my back as I release a playful squeal. Seth hovers over me, his lips a hair's breadth away from mine.

"It's your rules. I'm going to kiss you. If you don't want me to, just say the word." His warm breath skates over my lips.

My eyes search his, curious if he's actually going to kiss me. Because right now, that's the only thing on my mind. I lift my chin so my lips are just slightly closer to his. The movement an invitation and one he willingly accepts. His lips crash down to mine. My hands grip his biceps, needing to feel grounded. His tongue traces the crease of my lips, seeking entrance. I open, greeting his tongue with mine. My legs wrap around the back of his thighs and tug him closer so his body rests on mine. The bulge in his pants presses into the apex of my thighs. Thrusting upward, I grind myself against him and he releases a deep groan from the back of his throat. I do it again, loving that it drives him wild. Because it's exactly how I feel. Our tongues continue to caress one another's, slow and seductive. We continue grinding against each other like a couple of inexperienced teenagers. God, he makes me feel sixteen again. I can't get enough of him or enough of this or this with him. At this point, I don't even know anymore.

His hand skates across my bare stomach where my shirt has ridden up. His light touch sends a jolt of electricity coursing through my body. He pauses, unsure if he should continue his journey upward. I moan and grind against him, giving him the encouragement he needs. His lips find my column of my neck and he places a soft kiss there. The tips of his fingers roam up my torso until they reach the underside of my bra covered breast.

Suddenly both our phones start rapid fire dinging with message after message. Seth rests his forehead on my shoulder and mumbles, "Cock blocked by the phone."

"Sounds like we got service again."

Seth slowly sits up as he drags his hand from under my shirt. Instantly, I miss his warmth. Once his hand is free, he tugs my shirt back down to cover me up. I sit up, resting on my elbows.

"I guess we should let everyone know we're okay."

Seth runs his hands through his unruly hair. "Yeah, that's probably a good idea."

We both spend the next few minutes answering text messages and returning phone calls.

"I called the tow company. They can be here first thing in the morning to pull the car out and we can get back on the road," Seth says as he sits on the bed.

I look up from my phone. "Okay. That's great." A part of me is sad we'll be leaving our motel bubble. I don't remember the last time I've laughed so hard.

"Are you hungry? Shall we see what we can wrangle out of the vending machine?" Seth stands up and walks toward the door to slip on his shoes and jacket.

I give him a tight nod and hop off the bed to meet him by the door. He holds open my jacket so I can put my arms in the sleeves.

"Thanks," I mumble than gaze up into his face. The lust swirling in his irises makes me believe he's having the same thoughts as me, which are both of us naked and under the blanket.

We arrive back in the room with an arm full of snacks for our vending machine diet. I drop my haul on the bed and Seth does the same. We spend the next few minutes riffling through everything like kids with Halloween candy.

"I'll trade you a Ho-Ho for the peanut butter crackers." I hold out the chocolate and cream cake toward Seth.

Seth eyes the Ho-Ho and then the crackers. "Deal."

"You thought really hard about that." Seth tosses the crackers in my direction, and I catch them midair with two hands.

"I love these crackers."

"Same. They're my favorite." I open the package and hold out two of the crackers toward Seth. "I'll be nice and share." The biggest smile lights up his face as he takes the crackers.

We sit and eat our buffet for several minutes until Seth breaks the silence.

"So about earlier…" Uncertainty laces his voice.

"Yeah, about that… It was fun." I give him a tight-lipped smile.

"It was fun." His smile matches mine.

"But it can't be anything." I look down, my finger tracing a random pattern on the bedspread. If I look him in the eyes, he'll know I'm lying.

"But it could be something." He lifts my chin up with his finger, forcing me to look at him.

I want that, too. How I would love to just continue

where we left off earlier this afternoon, but it's Seth and he's a co-worker. "How about this…" I stare into his eyes, giving him a half truth. "What happens in the motel room, stays in the motel room. We have one more night here. Might as well make the most of it." I shrug one shoulder nonchalantly, secretly hoping he takes the bait because whatever magical superpowers he holds with his bow tie and glasses, I want more of it. Nervousness courses through me, unsure if this is something he wants as well. After several long seconds, his gaze sweeps up my body before his eyes lock onto mine. Lust and desire swirls in his eyes. He reaches across the bed and tugs on my arm, pulling me onto his lap.

"What happens in the motel, stays in the motel," he whispers across my lips. Then they meet mine in a bruising kiss. I wrap my arms around his neck as my fingers tangle in his locks that are just long enough to grab on to.

A moan escapes me as he tilts my head to deepen the kiss. His fingertips trail up my back under my shirt, the light touch sends goosebumps exploding over my body. Suddenly, he pulls away. I hope he doesn't regret this. He grips my hips and moves me off him. Shit. He regrets this. I try to hide the disappointment on my face. Seth rises to his knees and I'm convinced he's going to leave, but instead he swipes his hand across the bedspread, sending wrappers and vending machine snacks sailing across the room. Then he's tugging me down onto the comforter with him.

With Seth on top, his elbows resting on the side of my head, he's careful not to put his full weight on me. His eyes pinch tight at the sound of wrappers and snacks hitting the floor. A giggle escapes me knowing exactly what he's thinking. "You want to clean that up, don't you?"

"That was less satisfying than I was expecting." He

holds up his pointer finger as he hops off the bed and collects everything into a neat pile. The bed depresses when he climbs back on. A sexy smile covers his lips as he looks down at me. He reaches up to remove his black framed glasses.

I grip his wrist, stopping him. "Keep them on. They're hot."

A smile crosses his lips and I tug him the rest of the way down. His body blankets mine as we become a tangled mess of limbs. He peppers kisses along the column of my neck. I tilt my head to the side to give him better access.

"You smell like peaches. This might be my new favorite scent." His warm breath skates across my sensitive skin. He nuzzles his nose in the spot right behind my ear. "I bet you taste just as sweet as one, too."

I might just orgasm from his words alone. Lifting my hips, I grind myself against his thigh. Needing any type of friction I can get.

"There's only one way to find out," I blurt out. The thought of his mouth between my legs causes me to buck against him again. My hands roam over his back as I drag the hem of his shirt upward.

"That can be arranged." He stops his kissing assault to help me remove his shirt. This time, my hands wander over his lean-muscled shoulders and down his pecs, over the light tuft of chest hair, until they rest on his tapered waist.

His fingers grip the hem of my shirt and inches it upward, but he stops and looks at me for permission. My teeth dig into my bottom lip, and I give him a slight nod. He continues lifting until the hem is at the top of my breasts, leaving my pink lace bra exposed.

"You're beautiful." His eyes dart from my cleavage up to my face.

I can't help the smile that forms. "I don't think you're supposed to say that to a girl while you stare at her breasts."

"But they're very nice breasts." He gives me a wink before he bends down and places a kiss on the swell of my left breast. Then he moves to the other one. On instinct, I arch my back, needing him to keep going. His fingers hook the top of each cup and tug down, exposing my nipples to the cool air. Seth sucks one pebbled nipple into his mouth while his hand cups my other breast. His tongue swirls around the hard peak, occasionally giving it a light nip. The stimulation courses through my body as I writhe beneath him. As he continues to bite and suck on my breast, his other hand skims down my body until he reaches the elastic waistband of my flannel pajama pants. His fingers play with the fabric for a few seconds before he slips his hand inside. I thrust my hips up, encouraging him to continue. The anticipation killing me as if the slightest touch will cause me to detonate.

"Someone's eager," he mumbles around my nipple.

"You have no idea." I wiggle beneath him again, seeking any friction I can find. It's been longer than I'd like to admit since I've had sex. An orgasm, yes, I have those often but they've all been self-induced.

Then his fingers trail down and graze my clit over my lace panties. My legs spread farther to give him better access. He continues rubbing in small circles, varying the pressure, but I want more. Need more.

Taking control of the situation, I reach down and move my panties to the side so he knows exactly what I want and this time he gets the hint. He moves up to kiss me at the same time two of his fingers circle my clit, spreading the moisture around.

"You're so wet for me."

"Don't stop." I exhale a breathy moan from the sensation.

Two of his fingers plunge inside me. Needing more, I thrust my hips up, connecting with his hand. I grab the back of his head, fingers combing through his hair before I latch on, and bring his lips to mine. I want to feel him everywhere. His fingers continue to work themselves in and out of me, then he adds a third, stretching me even farther.

"Oh my God, that feels so good." Another moan escapes me.

He shifts his hand and while he moves in and out of me, his palm rubs against my clit. It's enough to send me over the edge. The buildup starts in my core. With each pump of his fingers and each rub against my clit causes a spark to ignite inside me. Suddenly, my entire body combusts into a blissful heat. His name erupts from my lips as my orgasm takes over. Eventually, his thrusting slows to a halt, then he removes his hand from my panties, and he rolls to the side. I fixate on his fingers as he brings them up to his mouth, sucking off my orgasm. He releases the last digit with a pop.

"Next time, I want to see what you taste like from between your legs."

I want that too. So bad. But I think I need to repay the orgasm. My gaze drifts down to the impressively large bulge tenting his sweats. Sitting up, I push on his shoulder until his back is flat on the mattress. I climb onto his lap, my butt resting on his thighs. The fair-haired scruff on his cheeks tickles the palms of my hands as I grab his face to kiss him, remnants of my taste still on his tongue. For a few minutes, our tongues mingle with each other. I pull away and move down his body until I reach his waistband. My fingers inch under the fabric, and I slowly pull down until his cock springs free and slaps against his belly. I tug his sweatpants down his legs until he's able to kick them free.

Seth sits up and leans back on his elbows to watch me. And I'm going to give him a show to watch. My fingers grip around the base. A bead of pre-cum glistens as I drag my tongue over the tip. I peer up at him through my lashes and stare into his hooded eyes, knowing he's enjoying the view. This time, I wrap my lips around the tip and slide down. When I pull back up, my hand gripping his cock follows. I continue the up and down motion, occasionally twisting my hand on the way up. A deep moan escapes Seth as his breathing picks up. He jerks his hips upward, hitting the back of my throat, and I swallow around the head. His hand tangles in my hair, lightly guiding me to move faster or to go deeper.

"Fuck. That feels so good. Don't stop. I'm going to come," Seth says in short pants.

I hum around his cock, the vibration sending him over the edge. His hot seed hits the back of my throat and I swallow him down. When he's finished, I sit back on my heels and wipe my mouth with my fingers. Seth lies there with his eyes closed for a few seconds before lifting one lid.

"That was amazing. Come here." He holds out his arms for me to crawl into. His arms wrap around me as he tugs the blanket over us. "Let's just lie here for a few minutes."

"I never expected you to be a cuddler." I rest my hand on his chest. His heartbeat still thumping erratically in his chest.

"You do that again and I'll do anything you want."

A giggle escapes me at his remark. We both lie there in silence. I'm snuggled up to his warm chest. I can't believe I just gave Seth a blow job. Forty-eight hours earlier I wanted to strangle him with his bow tie and now we're exchanging orgasms. Maybe it's the high altitude that's causing me to lose my mind. Do and think crazy thoughts. But this is our last night here. After tonight we go back to being Seth and Parisa who hate each other. Because nothing good can come from this if anyone finds out.

chapter eight
Tall Drink Of Handsome

Parisa

A soft light shining in through the curtain stirs me awake. Thoughts of last night replay in my mind. The way his fingers filled me. His soft lips on mine. The taste of him in my mouth. A part of me wants to do it all over again. I stretch my arm out to the other side of the bed. It's cold. When I open my eyes, my suspicions are confirmed. He's gone. I sit up and peer around the room for any sign of Seth. The bathroom door is open, so he's not in there. That's when I notice his jacket and shoes are missing. Several minutes later, the door opens, startling me. A few lone snowflakes blow in as Seth walks through the doorway.

"Where did you go?" I mentally scold myself for sounding so needy.

Seth shrugs out of his jacket and toes off his shoes. "I went and got the car so we can get back on the road. All the roads seem to be clear now, so we shouldn't have any issues."

"Oh. Okay. I'll just get my stuff packed." I climb out of bed and collect all my belongings from around the room. Seth does the same. The silence in the room is almost palpable.

After we finish loading the car, we drop our keys off at the front office and finish the rest of the drive to Aspen. Neither of us say a word about last night. But what's there to say? We agreed what happens at the motel would stay at the motel. I clench my thighs, just thinking about the way his fingers pumped in and out of me. Maybe it's not Seth I want, but the idea of him. Not him exactly, but a guy. It's been a really long time since I've had someone else's hands on my body. That must be it. I just needed to work out some sexual frustration and Seth just so happened to be there.

Within a few hours, we pull up to a massive ski resort nestled in the foothills of the Rocky Mountains. Seth drops me off under the overhang of the front entrance, along with our luggage to get checked in, while he parks the car in the underground parking garage. Seth meets me in the lobby and once we collect our room keys, I'm in room 902 while Seth has 810, we go our separate ways.

I slip the card into the reader and once the light turns green, I turn the handle and walk into one of the most gorgeous rooms I've ever stayed in. Huge floor to ceiling windows take up the exterior wall, giving me a stunning view of snowcapped mountains. A massive pillowtop king bed sits in the middle of the room with a gas fireplace next to a small sitting area. To the left is a spacious bathroom with granite counters and my very own soaking tub. *I will definitely make use of that tub before I leave.* On the right is a high-efficiency kitchenette. This studio room is better than my one-bedroom apartment back home.

When I'm all settled in, I call Mr. Evans to let him know we've made it. He said he'll email all the important information we'll need for the rest of the week and to meet him in the lobby in the morning before the panels start for the day. I throw on some comfy clothes and crawl on top of the luxurious mattress. This is way better than The Pine Needle Motel From Hell. I pull out my laptop and go over the email Mr. Evans sent, along with notes for my marketing presentation later this week. This promotion is mine. I can almost taste it. After several hours, exhaustion takes over my body. Closing my computer, I set it on the nightstand. I tug the blanket over me, realizing this bed is entirely too big for one person.

The next morning, I find Seth already waiting for Mr. Evans in the lobby. Of course, he would be the first to arrive. His hair is perfectly styled, his navy suit pristinely pressed. I bet he woke up early and ironed it himself. No, scratch that, I'm sure he did it last night before hanging it up in the closet. His outfit wouldn't be complete without his signature bow tie. As I step closer, I notice he's gone a more subtle route with pink stripes as opposed to the alligator print from last week.

I drop my bag next to the chair across from him and plop down onto the hard cushion. For a fancy hotel, I was expecting something a little softer. I cross one leg over the other and rub the back of my thigh. When I look up, Seth's eyes are watching my hand as I caress the sore spot.

His gaze finally lifts to meet mine and I quirk an eyebrow at him.

His gaze quickly returns to the papers in front of him as he clears his throat. "Often businesses will purposely purchase uncomfortable furniture so patrons don't get too comfortable and occupy the space for long periods of time. This is most common in restaurants."

"Well, thanks for that tidbit of information." I try to keep the snarkiness out of my tone, but fail. *That's all he has to say to me? Why do I even bother?*

Just then, Mr. Evans arrives to brief us on today's panels and asks if we have any questions. After the brief meeting, we make our way to the first of several panels for the day.

After lunch, Seth and I prepare our presentations on how to take Blue Stone Group's marketing to the next level. This is what I've worked my ass off for. I nail this presentation and the Marketing Director position is mine. Having this position would mean paying off my student loans, paying off my car, getting out of my crappy one-bedroom apartment, and I could even afford a nice luxury vacation.

There are about twenty of us seated at a long table in a conference room. Seth is at the head of the table as he prepares his presentation. Once he's ready, the room quiets down. He taps a few keys on his computer and a PowerPoint presentation lights up the screen behind him. Of course, he would have this perfect presentation using modern technology. Here I am with my poster board diagrams like I'm in fifth grade. I'm an idiot. As he presents his ideas to the board, I can't help but admire his confidence and poise, albeit a bit stiff at times. He knows how to demand the attention of a room. And I must admit he has some great ideas that I wish I had thought of.

Once Seth finishes, he flashes everyone a dazzling smile and packs up his things. As I stand, my heart feels like it's going to thump out of my chest. I inconspicuously wipe the sweat from my palms on my skirt when I bend down to collect my items for the presentation. I set up my poster boards on the easels while everyone talks amongst themselves. When I face the table, I'm instantly greeted by a pair of familiar green eyes staring back at me while a smile tugs at the corner of his lips. Just from that look, heat creeps up the back of my neck. Quickly, I turn back around, needing to collect my thoughts, get my mind back into this presentation and off *him*. I inhale a deep breath and slowly exhale and put on my game face.

When I'm finished with my presentation, I'm greeted with a small round of applause before everyone disperses from the room. I begin to pack up my stuff when I sense a presence behind me. I turn around and Seth is leaning against the table, hands gripping the sides.

"You gave a great presentation. Everyone loved your display."

"Thanks. You too. You had some really great ideas."

His eyes stare down at his feet before they come back up to meet mine. "Everyone is meeting down in the bar for drinks. If you want to go."

"Uh, yeah. Sure. I'm just going to finish packing up and I'll head down there."

"Great. I'll see you later then."

"Yeah. See you later."

With that, Seth stands and strolls out of the conference room. I watch his every step until he exits the doorway. Maybe the bar isn't a good idea?

When I walk into the hotel bar, the place is packed. People mill around, socializing. I walk up to the bar and grab a drink before I find a pub table to sit at. My eyes dart around the room to see if I find anyone I recognize. Who am I kidding? Seth. I'm looking for Seth. Soon after, Jamie, a girl I met earlier, joins me. We chat about the conference and where we work. She does marketing at a different real estate development firm in Illinois.

"Who's that tall drink of handsome standing over there? The one with the bow tie."

As soon as she mentions the bow tie, I instantly know who she's talking about, but my gaze follows hers anyway. "That's Seth. We work together in the same office. He's annoying as hell with his know-it-all attitude." I take a sip of my drink and the next words tumble out of my mouth. "You like the bow tie?"

She bites her bottom lip with her eyes still trained on Seth. "In a room full of ties, he has the confidence to wear a bow tie. A pink one, in fact." Her eyes come to mine. "That's sexy as hell. Do you know if he has a girlfriend?"

After what we did at the motel, I hope he's doesn't. I'd rather not add home wrecker to my resume. "Far as I know, he's single," I reply.

"I think I'll go see if he wants a drink. Then hopefully later he'll tie me up using one of those bow ties." She winks as she sets down her drink and saunters to where Seth is talking to a couple of other guys.

When she reaches the group, she introduces herself with a handshake while the other two guys walk off. I can't hear what they're saying, but the way she throws her head back with laughter makes me believe she's just being over the top because there is no way Seth is that funny. Her hand brushes down his bicep. His eyes wander to where she's touching him, then he looks to her, a crinkle in the corner of his eyes. A smile graces both their lips. That look has me gripping my glass so hard I'm surprised it doesn't shatter under my fingertips. I throw back the rest of my drink before I stomp to the bar to get a new one, needing all the alcohol I can get to make it through this night.

Several hours later, I'm back at the table from mingling when the familiar smell of citrus and cedar assaults my nose.

His voice, a whisper across the shell of my ear, sends goosebumps down my arms. "Having fun?" He takes the seat next to me.

I shift my gaze to meet his. Tilting my head, my lips pull into a small smile. "I was until you sat down."

He releases a small chuckle. We sit in silence for a moment as we each take a sip of our drinks. Don't ask him. Don't ask him. "So, where's Jamie?" *Shit.* He looks at me quizzically, unsure of who I'm referring to. "The brunette who was groping your arm earlier."

Recognition covers his face. "Oh, her. Yeah, she really wanted to see what I looked like wearing a bow tie… naked." Pink flushes his cheeks.

I can't help the humor in my voice. "Is that so?"

"Yeah. But I told her my bow ties are reserved for only one special woman, so she went on her merry way. I'm sure she'll find some other unsuspecting victim to hook up with." His eyes meet mine for a moment, the intensity so strong I'm surprised I don't combust right in my chair. "But I think I'm going to call it a night. Long day of travel tomorrow." He sets his drink down and before I can say a word, he's out the door.

Soon after Seth left, I finished my drink and followed suit. Now, I'm lying in this massive bed all by myself with thoughts of Seth roaming through my mind. I try everything to distract myself from my own thoughts. I turn on the TV but a commercial for glasses comes on and I can't help but think of Seth and the way his eyes glint behind his black rimmed glasses. Then I try reading my book, but the hero used his neck tie to tie the heroine to the headboard. Then images of Seth's lean, muscular frame hovering over me as he ties me up using his bow tie flit through my mind. I slam my e-reader to the bed. Maybe I just need to work out some sexual tension. Again. Yeah, that must be it.

My hand dips into the waistband of my sleep pants while my other cups my breast. I pinch my hardened nipple as my fingers massage my clit. I work to find a rhythm as I thrust my finger in and out. But this isn't what I want. These aren't the hands I want on my body. Fuck.

Pulling my hand from under the blanket, I drop it onto the bed and sigh in frustration. I know what I want. I just wonder if he's thinking the same thing.

chapter nine

Wolf In Sheep's Clothing

Seth

The whole evening, I would sneak glances in her direction, hoping she wouldn't see me. I don't know what it is about Parisa that has me in knots. She tests my limits on the best of days and yet I can't get enough. The way she mumbles to herself when she's frustrated or when she rewards herself on a job well done with a small lollipop. Let me say, it gets hard to concentrate when she wraps her lips around sugary candy and sucks.

Now I'm lying in bed, imagining her in here with me, her lips wrapped around my cock like back at the motel. My dick swells at the memory. Why the hell did we decide to never do that again? That was the stupidest idea ever. I run my hand down my stomach and into my boxer briefs. If I can't have her, this will have to do. My fingers wrap around my shaft, giving it a firm squeeze before tugging up. I repeat the process and I imagine it's Parisa's hand giving me pleasure.

While mid-stroke, a knock forces me to pause. Was that on my door? I hold my breath, waiting for the sound again so I can pinpoint where it's coming from. Just then, another soft knock sounds and this time I know it's on my door. I reply that I'll be there in a minute. Jumping out of bed, I frantically scan the room for my sweatpants. After I tug them on, I peer through the peephole and catch sight of Parisa on the other side, pacing the narrow hallway. With just one look at her I'm biting back the smile on my face while my cock twitches with delight. *Let's see what she wants first before we get overly excited.* I turn the handle and open the door a crack.

"Hey, what's up?"

She stops her pacing and looks up at me with uncertainty etched behind her hazel eyes. Then those hazel eyes drift down as she takes in my cotton covered chest and gray sweatpants before snapping back up to mine. "You know what? Never mind. This is a bad idea. Just forget I stopped by." She turns on her heel to walk away, but I catch her wrist before she can leave. Her eyes fixate where I'm touching her, but I don't want to let her go.

"What did you want?" My voice is soft, so I don't scare her away. When she looks back up at me, I release her wrist.

Her teeth dig into her bottom lip, contemplating what to say. In a single breath, she says, "You know how we said that what happens at the motel, stays at the motel?"

"Yeah?"

Her gaze fixates on the geometric pattern in the carpet before lifting to meet my eyes. "What if we change that to what happens in Colorado, stays in Colorado?"

I can't help the wide grin that covers my face. "Change your mind?"

"Ugh! Don't be so smug. I just wanted a quiet night to myself, but then there was a commercial on TV that reminded me of you. Then the hero in my book ties which is close to a bow tie and they were about to do some sexy things. Again, I pictured you and me doing those things like back at the motel. And I hate you because I can't stop thinking about you."

I step into her space and cup her cheeks. Leaning down, I press my lips to hers to shut her up. Slowly, I pull away, my lips centimeters away from hers. "Do you want to come in?"

With my hands still grasping her cheeks, she eagerly nods her head. This time when I grab her wrist, it's to pull her into my room. I slam the door behind her and press her back to it. My hands cup her cheeks as my mouth slants over hers. Our kiss is tender at first, but growing more demanding as each second passes. Her hands grip my waist to pull me closer. Desire courses through my body. All I wanted was one more night with this girl and now here she is, in my room, my body pressed against hers. I move my hands from her cheeks to thread my fingers through her soft hair. Turning us around, I walk her backwards, my lips still fused to hers. When her knees hit the edge of the bed, she falls backward and sinks into the mattress. Gripping the back of my shirt, I pull it over my head. Her hooded eyes watch me as she nibbles on her bottom lip.

"Get over here." She motions with her finger.

That's all the invitation I need. She scoots up the bed as I crawl over her body. Her legs spread and I nestle between them, my hard cock pressing against her hot core. Gently, I thrust against her, and a needy moan escapes her lips. Her hands grip my waist, guiding my motion as she lifts her hips to press into me, the friction driving both of us wild.

"Fuck. I want you so bad right now." I pepper kisses along her jaw and down her neck.

"Then what are you waiting for?"

Good question. I sit up and stare down at this beautiful woman laying on my bed. Her auburn locks fanned out across the comforter. Desire swirls in her irises. Then it hits me.

"I don't have a condom. I wasn't expecting to have sex on this trip."

"Shit." Her hands fall to the mattress.

"There's a little gift shop in the lobby. They must have condoms."

"Yeah, probably twenty dollars for a pack of three."

"Twenty dollars spent now is much more reasonable than two hundred thousand for the next eighteen years."

"Fair enough."

"I'll be right back." I hop off the bed and throw my shirt back on.

"You might want to do something to contain the beast." Parisa nods toward my achingly stiff dick.

I look down. Shit. "Good call." I rifle through the closet where I hung up my clothes and pluck a hoodie off the hanger, pulling it over my head. That will hopefully help conceal my hard on or at least make it a little less conspicuous. "I'll be right back. Don't finish without me." I flash her a bright smile and she laughs, the sound making my dick twitch. With one last glance at Parisa, I reluctantly close the door behind me and haul ass down the hallway to the elevators.

When the doors open at the lobby level, I exit to the small hallway and glance left, then right. As soon as I spot the small gift shop, I make a mad dash to the door. Upon entering the small space, I see a wall of over-the-counter medications and then behind the register are a few small boxes of condoms. I stroll up to the counter and let the girl know what I want. Just then, another person enters the shop.

"Seth. I thought that was you."

I whirl around at the sound of my name. Damn it. My neck flames when I see who it is. "Hi, Mr. Evans. What are you doing down here?"

"Heartburn. The curry chicken was delicious but I'm paying the price now. I forgot my meds at home, so I thought I would see what they have here. How about yourself?"

"Your total is eighteen dollars and thirty-one cents," the girl behind the counter says.

Mr. Evans eyes the box on the counter, then his gaze shifts back to me. A sly smile plays on his lips. "Well, you have a good night, Seth. Great job on your presentation today."

Mr. Evans clasps my shoulder, then continues his journey to the wall of heartburn medications. I pinch my eyes closed for a brief second, realizing my boss knows I'm about to have sex. I pull my wallet from my pocket and hand over my card for her to run. When she's finished, I grab the box and hightail it out of the store and back toward the elevators. I press the up button and wait and wait and wait until finally a set of doors behind me opens. Once inside, I press the button for the eighth floor and then press the close door button. My patience is running out. I just want to get back to Parisa so we can finish what we started. I watch the floor numbers increase... two... three... four. The elevator stops, and the doors open and fuck my life. The girl from the bar earlier, Jamie, I think, stands on the other side. A smile lights up her face as she walks into the elevator and stands next to me. She reaches over and presses the button for the tenth floor.

"So, it looks like you're in for a fun night."

"Why do you say that?"

She nods toward my hand still holding the box of condoms. Dammit. I tuck the box into my hoodie pocket.

"Uh, yeah."

"I assume it's with another person. Can't say I know anyone who masturbates with a condom on, but maybe it saves from cleaning up a mess. Either way, it's none of my business."

Luckily for me, the doors open for my floor, and I can't get out of the elevator fast enough. "Have a good night," I quickly say over my shoulder just as the doors close. Who else could I possibly run into before I make it to my door? Maybe I should have taken my chances without the condom. I would have saved myself the embarrassment at least.

When I get back to the room, Parisa is sitting up in bed, leaning against the headboard. I toss the box of condoms on the comforter and flop down on my back next to her.

"What's wrong?"

"Embarrassment." I throw my forearm over my eyes.

"What happened?"

"First, Mr. Evans popped into the gift shop at the same time I did and now knows I'm about to have sex. Then I had to share an elevator with the girl from the bar earlier this evening, who also knows I'll be having sex after I turned her down."

"So, a couple of people are fully aware you are about to get lucky tonight. We better give them one hell of a story, then." She straddles my lap, cups my cheeks, and presses her soft lips to mine.

I relish in the feel of her body on top of mine. Her kiss is delicate at first, then becomes firmer, more demanding. All my embarrassment is tossed out the window. My hands trail up her back, hugging her closer to me. Just when she thinks she's the one in control, in one swift motion, I flip her over so I'm on top. She playfully squeals at the sudden change of position.

"Now, where were we?" I press a kiss to her swollen lips, then trail down the column of her neck. I drag the collar of her shirt over her shoulder and place kisses on her collarbone. My fingers clasp the sides of her shirt and slowly drag it over her torso, past her ribs, and over her lace covered breasts. I sit up, allowing both of us space so I can finish removing her shirt along with her bra. Next, I quickly drag her yoga pants down her smooth legs, taking her panties with them in the process. I give myself a few moments to admire this stunning woman lying in my bed, waiting for me. How in the hell did I get so lucky? A smile tugs at my lips.

"What's the smile for?"

"You."

I climb off the bed and remove my hoodie and shirt. I saunter to the closet and grab the three bow ties I packed. When I return, I toss them on the bed. Parisa sits up, resting on her elbows, her eyebrows drawn together.

"What are you doing?"

"Tying you up." I hook my thumbs into the waistband of my sweatpants and tug them down. Parisa's gaze zeros in on my movements and she bites her lips as my cock bobs up and down in front of her.

"With bow ties?"

"They're more useful than you think." I clench the bow

ties in one hand as I crawl onto the bed over her body. She takes the hint and lies down on her back.

"I never expected you to be into kink."

"You'd be surprised." I wrap one bow tie around her left wrist, securing the knot, then I do the same with the right. Grabbing both her wrists, I haul them over her head and use the third bow tie to secure the two together. "Now, I'm out of bow ties, so if you don't keep quiet, I'll have to stuff your mouth with something else to shut you up."

She firmly presses her lips together and nods. I grab the bow tie that links the two connected to her wrists and tug up, causing her arms to fully stretch above her head. Her eyes go wide for a moment before lust takes over.

"I think I'm going to like this."

"Trust me, I *know* you're going to like this. But if at any time you don't or it's uncomfortable, let me know, okay?" She nods her head. "I need words. Tell me you understand."

"I understand."

Keeping her arms taut above her head, I bring my lips to hers in a demanding kiss. I probe the seam with my tongue, seeking entrance, and she willingly opens up for me. Our tongues stroke and caress each other's while my free hand mimics the movements over her right breast. My fingertips pinch her nipple until it's a hard peak. Her body bucks off the bed beneath me with each pinch while her sweet moans echo around the room. I lightly trail my fingertips down her body as I pull away from our kiss. Gazing down, I watch as goosebumps explode across her skin. Once my hand reaches the apex of her thighs, I use my fingers to spread her open. Her body writhes beneath me as her chest rises and falls with her heavy pants. I brush my middle finger down her slick entrance before pushing in.

"Oh fuck. Seth. Yes. I need more." Her voice is a sweet plea.

"No worries. I'll be giving you more in just a second."

I push my finger in and out of her opening before adding a second finger, my speed increasing with every moan she gives me. Finally, I'm adding a third and she bucks her hips, meeting my hand thrust for thrust. A small whimper escapes her when I pull my fingers out. I bring them up to my mouth and suck her orgasm off each digit.

"I've tasted you from my fingers, but I think it's time I get a taste from the source." Pushing her knees apart, I place kisses down her inner thigh until I reach her pussy, then I repeat the action on the other side. Her body squirms beneath me, and her moans fill the room. I love how the slightest touch makes her wild.

"Seth. I need you." Her hips jut off the bed as I run my teeth over the tender flesh of her thigh.

"What do you need?"

"You. Your tongue. Fucking me." She exhales in deep pants.

"Only because you've been a good girl." Before she can say anything else, I run the tip of my tongue along her slit, her sweet arousal coating my tongue. And I want more. I lap at her juices like a starved man, flicking my tongue over her clit. Her moans and whimpers fill the room. It's a sound I've come to very much enjoy. I probe her entrance, tongue fucking her like she asked. Her legs tremble beside my head, her breathing shallow as I suspect she's about to come again. Her tied hands reach down, and her fingers comb through my hair before she grasps my strands and holds tight while she rides out her first orgasm. Finally, her grip loosens, and I sit up and wipe her arousal off my face with the back of my hand.

"That was amazing. Why didn't we do this earlier?" She looks up at me with hooded eyes.

"Just wait. I have something better for you."

I reach across the bed and tear into the box of condoms. I pull out a foil packet and rip it open, rolling the rubber down my thick cock and positioning myself between her thighs. With one hand, I grab the bow ties, stretching her arms above her head again, and use my other to guide my cock to her entrance. Slowly, I push into her, her body sucking me in. She releases another throaty moan. I pinch my eyes closed, loving the way I feel inside of her. Her core clenches around the intrusion, sending another jolt of pleasure through my body.

"Fucking hell. Your pussy feels so good wrapped around my dick."

I slowly pump in and out of her, letting her body adjust to my size, but soon after, my speed picks up and I'm slamming into her. Her moans fill the room, mixed with the slapping of our bodies as they come together. After a few more thrusts, I'm pulling out. I tug on the bow ties forcing her to sit up. Her hair a wild mess as I stare into her hooded eyes.

"I'm going to flip you over so you're on your knees. That okay?"

She nods and I press a kiss to her lips before rolling her over and positioning her on her knees, elbows resting on the bed. I grab the soft flesh of her hips and slam into her from behind. She releases a yelp of surprise before it quickly turns to a moan. I piston in and out of her, driving deep with each thrust. I reach around her and grab the bow ties and tug down so her cheek hits the comforter. Her round ass sticking up even higher causes my thrusts to go even deeper.

"Oh god. Seth. O-oh. Fuck. That feels so good."

Her moans and whimpers spur me to go faster and harder. My hand goes to her clit, my fingers rub in rhythmic strokes while I continue to pump in and out. A bead of sweat trickles down my back. A few moments later, I can feel her clench around me, body trembling as she moans out my name. Just then I feel a tingle in my lower back while my balls seize up and my orgasm takes over my body. I drive deeper with each thrust until I erupt, my orgasm filling the condom. My movements slow and eventually stop. While still inside her I reach around and release the bow tie that was linking her two hands together. When she's free, she lifts herself up so she's positioned on all fours. I slowly pull out and she whimpers from the loss.

"Let me get you cleaned up."

I press a kiss to the dimples right above her butt before crawling off the bed. Pulling off the condom, I discard it in the bathroom trash can. I grab a washcloth and run it under warm water for her. When I return to the main room, she's still in the same position I left her, and fuck me, I like the sight. I run the warm cloth over her sensitive skin before tossing it into the plastic laundry bag of dirty towels. I pull back the covers and she lays down on the bed on her side and I follow suit facing her, tugging the blanket over us.

"You're the epitome of a wolf in sheep's clothing. I don't think I've had an orgasm quite like that before."

"Me either. Also, I wouldn't be opposed to doing that again." Her eyes meet mine as my lips tip up into a smile.

A blush creeps over her cheeks. Looking for a distraction, she runs her fingers over the silky fabric. "So, what's up with you and these bow ties? Most guys just wear a tie, but not you."

I draw lazy circles on her hand where the bow ties are

still on her wrists. "Never underestimate a guy in a bow tie."

She releases a small chuckle. "Clearly. And who knew they were so versatile?"

I make quick work to free her wrists from the cloth. "Neck ties are a piece a fabric that ties around your neck and dangles from your body. It can get caught in machines, paper shredders, conveyor belts. I'll have you know, you're twice as likely to die from a necktie than you are from getting attacked by a shark."

Her gaze flits up to mine. Disbelief in her voice. "Shut up! You're lying."

"No joke. On average, ten people die annually from necktie related accidents. So, bow ties are short and close to my body. No worries about accidental strangulation."

"Huh. Who knew?" She continues to play with my bow tie. "Can you teach me how to tie one?"

"Sure, but later. I'm comfortable and I'm not ready to let you go just yet."I tighten my grip on her as I nuzzle her neck, inhaling her sweet peach scent.

We both lie there for several minutes, enjoying the warmth of the other person. But Parisa being as restless as she is, climbs out of bed, her naked body on display as she scoops up one of my t-shirts draped over a chair and pulls it over her head. She looks tiny wearing my shirt. The hem just kisses the back of her thighs.

She saunters to the full-length mirror, bow tie in hand. Her delicate fingers wrap the silky fabric around her neck, her brows furrow as she concentrates on figuring out how to tie it. A wide grin covers my face as I watch her determination. After she struggles for several minutes, I toss my legs over the side of the bed, throw on a pair of boxer briefs, and meet her at the mirror. My eyes lock onto her hazel ones in the mirror as my fingers skate up her bare arms, causing goosebumps to cover her flesh. Her lips part as she inhales a sharp breath.

Bending down, I trail kisses up the side of her neck. I whisper into the shell of her ear, "The trick is you need one side longer than the other, otherwise you end up with a lopsided bow." My fingers rest on hers as I guide them to tie the perfect bow tie. When we're finished, my hands skim down her body and rest on her waist. A beaming smile covers her face as she turns to face me. Her arms snake around the back of my neck, her fingers tickle the short hairs there.

"I have to say this pink bow tie looks pretty good on me."

"It looks hot." My lips capture hers in a brief kiss. When we break apart, her face falls as her gaze lands on the floor. "Hey, what's wrong?" I lift her chin so she's forced to look at me. Her eyes search mine before answering.

"We go home tomorrow. I've enjoyed this little cocoon we've been in for the past few days." She pulls away and moves to sit on the edge of the bed. Her fingers tug on the end of the bow tie, the fabric falling to her lap. "Back to reality, I guess."

The bed dips as I sit beside her. "This doesn't have to end."

"Yes, it does. It's already gone on longer than it should. Hell, it shouldn't have even started."

"But you couldn't resist my rugged good looks and charismatic charm?" She lets out a small laugh. God, I love that sound.

"Call it a moment of weakness."

Now it's my turn to laugh.

"I think it's best we just leave everything here. We can

go back to hating each other once we get back home." Her eyes meet mine.

All I can do is nod. If I try to convince her otherwise, I might just end up pushing her away. But something has her hesitant to pursue this. On the best of days, we hate each other, but I'm drawn to her. And since I've had a taste, I never want to lose her. Right now, I guess I'll take her any way I can have her.

"We're not home yet," I twist and cup her face as I brush my thumb over her soft cheek, "so why don't we spend whatever time we have left enjoying each other's company?"

She nuzzles into my palm. "I like that idea. How do you feel about bubble baths? Because there is a giant soaker tub over there that I'm dying to try out."

chapter ten

Don't Date The Coworkers

My bed is cold and lonely without Seth next to me. Ugh! Why can't I get him out of my head? Sure, he gave me several days of mind-blowing orgasms, which I really didn't think he had in him, but he certainly proved me wrong. Now I'm back in Minnesota, back in my empty bed, staring at the dark ceiling, and the only thing I want is Seth. Thoughts of his hands roaming my body and his mouth between my legs, doing that thing with his tongue again, float through my mind. Damn. It's been way too long since a man touched me like that, probably my last boyfriend at my previous job.

Once again, I scold myself. Don't date the coworkers. That should be the cardinal rule, and clearly one I can't follow. But I'm not dating Seth. It's just sex. It was only sex.

He could have been any faceless guy, and I'm sure I would have the same feelings. The sex induced endorphins must still be coursing through my body. That's it. This will pass. I turn to my side and stare at the blue digital numbers of my alarm clock. But what if I don't want it to pass?

Several restless hours later, my alarm goes off and I amble out of bed. I do my best to put myself together for work, but I'm sure I look like I was on an all night bender. By the time I'm pushing through the door of The Blue Stone Group, I'm ready to go back home. Not only am I tired but I'm anxious about seeing Seth. My heartbeat pounds in my throat as I trudge toward the front desk where Olivia and Charlie are seated.

"I don't want this to sound harsh, but you look like hell," Olivia says.

"No, I get it. I didn't get any sleep last night."

"That because of the trip to Colorado?" Charlie asks.

My eyes go wide as my hands become clammy. "Why? Why would you say that?" I blurt out faster than necessary.

"You got home late Saturday, so I'm sure you didn't get much time to unwind. And the hour time change doesn't help." Charlie furrows her brow at me.

"Oh. Yeah. That must be the reason I couldn't sleep last night. I'll make up for the lack of sleep tonight. Go to bed early."

"I'm going to go on a coffee run on break. Want me to get you something?" Charlie asks.

"That would be amazing. Thank you." Just as I turn around to walk toward the elevator, Seth strolls through the glass doors. His gray suit is perfectly tailored to fit his broad shoulders and narrow waist. When my gaze wanders back up, I'm met with a pair of familiar eyes behind black rimmed glasses. He offers a nod, and I can't help but notice the slight upturn to his lips. Heat creeps up my neck knowing he knows what I look like under my clothes. Excitement courses through me because I also know what he looks like under his.

"So how was the conference, Parisa? We heard about the airport mishap and getting stuck in a blizzard." Olivia tilts her head at me like she's trying to read my thoughts.

"It was… good," I lie. I lie so hard because it was more than good. Like I can't stop thinking about it. But I can't tell them. I can't tell anyone. Plus, we said what happened in Colorado stays in Colorado and Seth agreed, so this is what he wants too.

Just the thought of him gives me heart palpitations, and I really want to get to my desk and see him. I make plans with Olivia and Charlie to meet at Porter's later and then I scurry to the elevator. My heart beats louder with each passing second as I anticipate seeing Seth again. When I round the corner to where our desks sit, my gaze darts to his first and my heart sinks. All that sits at his desk is an empty chair. I take a closer peek, thinking maybe he's using the restroom or something, but there's no sign that Seth has come to his cubical yet. His computer screen is black, his chair is pushed in, not a pen is out of place. Finally, I take a seat at my desk and distract myself with work.

Throughout the entire morning, the scuffle of feet passing my desk would cause me to look up to see if it's Seth, and each time I'm disappointed. What has he done to me? I've never been like this.

Suddenly, the hairs on the back of my neck stand up. Then the familiar scent of citrus and cedar wafts around me and instantly I know it's him and my lips split into a smile. His chair squeaks as he pulls it back from his desk and takes a seat. My cheeks flame as I sense his eyes on me.

I'm fighting to show him I haven't been waiting to see him all morning, but I'm failing miserably.

From the corner of my eye, I watch as Seth turns toward his desk and scribbles something on the piece of paper, then slowly slides it across our shared half wall. My gaze wanders down, then back up to meet his and he nods at the folded note.

I peer behind me like a teenager trying not to get caught passing notes by the teacher before I grab the folded paper. My fingers fumble as I open it and read the short, right slanted words.

You're all I've thought about all weekend.

My gaze lingers over his words. I never knew seven words could affect me this way. Grabbing one of the several pens scattered on my desk, I jot down a reply, fold the note, and slide it back to him. While he unfolds the note, I prop my chin on my hands. His jaw drops and I know he read what I wrote. He twists toward me, a glint of lust swirls behind his irises causing me to clench my thighs together, needing a little friction to take the edge off. He pulls his gaze away from mine and scribbles something down before passing the note back to me.

Quickly, I grab it and unfold the now worn paper.

Since I made you wet all weekend from thinking about me, what do you say we go take care of that?

Shit. My thighs clench together all over again. I peer at him through my lashes and he's watching me with intent. Just as my pen hits the paper, a deep voice from behind startles me, causing me to jump, and my pen drops to the floor.

"Seth, Parisa. I need to see both of you in my office." I swivel around, picking up my pen in the process, as Mr. Evans stands behind me sipping coffee from his mug that reads *Monday's are for Winners*.

Clearing my throat, I tell him, "Okay. We'll be right there." Mr. Evans turns and disappears around the corner. Seth rises to his feet at the same time as me.

chapter eleven

T.W.A.T. Closet

Parisa

After our brief meeting with Mr. Evans, we head back to our desks. We were told how impressed he was with our presentations, and we've made the decision a very difficult one for the board, but we should hear back soon about their choice. I want this promotion so bad. I need this promotion. I've put in so many hours of extra work and after what happened at my last job, I need this for my own self-worth. I deserve this. But then there's Seth, who wants this promotion not only for himself but to help his family. And that right there has me torn. We both deserve it, but one is going to be disappointed. That thought sours my entire mood.

I dive into my work, hoping I can distract myself. Several minutes pass, until out of the corner of my eye, a folded piece of paper resting on top of the half cubicle wall catches my attention. I glance behind me to make sure no one is watching before I snatch it and unfold the paper.

What has you looking so sad?

It's crazy to think how well he can read me. Even without me saying anything, he just knows. I contemplate telling him the truth or just making something up. I decide on the latter. So, I jot something down.

Feeling a little fatigued. I skipped breakfast this morning and the coffee just isn't cutting it.

I pass the note back to him. From the corner of my eye, I watch as he unfolds the paper and reads my words. Then he's bending down, opening a drawer in his desk, and placing a granola bar on top of the wall. Unable to fight it, my lips tug into a smile. I mouth *thank you* and snag the granola bar. He really makes it hard to hate him when he does things like this. A moment later, another note is sitting on the wall. Unfolding the paper, I read what he wrote.

My watch is still on mountain time, and I know of an empty storage closet.
What do you say? Circle: Yes or No

A laugh bubbles out of me before I write my response.

Is that the reason for the granola bar?
To make sure I have enough energy.

I fold the paper and pass it back to him. It only takes a few seconds before he's passing it back to me and I read it.

Dual motives. One to make sure you eat and then the selfish one. So, what do you say.
Yes or No

A shy smile pulls at my lips. I feel like I'm sixteen years old again, crushing on the cute guy in class. I circle my choice before folding the paper back into its original shape and slide it toward Seth. He takes the paper, unfolds it, and a wide grin covers his face. He replies with another message and folds the paper again to give back. This time his words are directions on a time and place to meet him.

A few seconds later, Seth stands and saunters past me. I watch as he disappears around the corner. Once he's out of sight, I stare at the clock in the upper right-hand corner of my computer screen, willing it to move faster. As soon as it hits the five-minute mark, I'm out of my seat and leaving in the same direction Seth went.

When I reach the elevator, I hit the button for the lower level and pray that no one else needs an elevator because I don't think I can wait for a stop. When the doors open, I'm in the basement. The fluorescent lighting is much harsher and the white walls give the space a sterile feel. To the right is a bunch of old real estate signs and boxes of who knows what. Next to that is a wall of file cabinets filled with old paperwork from before things went digital. Then in the middle of a short hallway with a stairwell at the end, is the room Seth told me about. My heels echo off the bare walls with each footfall.

Within a few strides, I'm standing in front of the door. Did Seth want me to knock? Walk right in? I go with the first. Just as I lift my hand the door flies open, and a hand reaches for my wrist and tugs me inside. Before I know it, Seth pushes me until my back hits the door, then his lips are on mine.

My hands fly up, gripping his suspenders for support. His hands wrap around my waist and tugs me closer to him as he nips at my bottom lip. Then his lips are back on mine in a bruising kiss. Hard and demanding, like he can't get enough of me. I part my lips for him and our tongues caress each other's, soft and sensual.

Suddenly, the door is shoved open. The handle jabs me in the hip as a sliver of light peeks in from the hallway before our weight slams the door shut. We both freeze, unsure of who's on the other side of the door. Then the door opens again, but this time Seth closes it with his hand.

I can hear whispered voices on the other side of the door followed by a soft knock. Seth directs me to the side as he opens the door a crack.

"What do you want?"

"What are you doing in the twat closet?" Bennett's voice sounds through the crack.

"The twat closet?"

"T.W.A.T. The Weekday Adult Time Closet."

I cover my mouth with both hands, trying to hold back my laughter as they banter back and forth about the closet's name.

"I don't know. That's what Trey came up with, and I didn't have the energy to argue. But also, don't deflect the question."

"I'm just hanging out. Need some time to myself."

"Time to yourself only means one thing. Are you doing a little hand to gland combat? You know this isn't the time or place to be doing something like that."

"Oh yeah and having sex with Charlie is? Go find somewhere else. Like your office."

"Needed a change of scenery."

"Well, this room is occupied."

"Fine. Just be sure to clean up after yourself. Also, Porter's tonight?"

"Got it."

Seth closes the door and leans his head against the cool wood. I move to stand next to him as my hand caresses his arm. "So, is that how you know about this room? Come down here to relieve a little tension?" I ask, unable to hold a straight face.

"No. I had to come down here to drop off a box and found it to be a quiet space if I needed a few minutes. Unfortunately, I made the mistake of mentioning it to Bennett and Trey and they took it upon themselves to defile my quiet space."

"Do you think Bennett suspects you were in here with someone?"

"I think he was too preoccupied with your friend to notice."

"I still can't believe those two are dating. And I forgot, Charlie and Olivia invited me out to Porter's as well."

"With our friends now dating, I suppose it's only natural for the two groups to become one."

I inhale a deep breath and lean against the door and bite my lower lip. "Yeah, I suppose."

My heart thunders in my chest at the thought of my two best friends, who know me better than anyone, all hanging out together with Seth, the guy I'm secretly banging. Shit.

chapter twelve
Something's In The Water

Seth

"You know what the world is missing?" Trey takes a gulp of his beer before setting the pint glass down on the table.

The crowd at Porter's is quieter tonight, but there are still plenty of people milling around. My foot bounces on the bottom of the barstool, anticipating Parisa's arrival. It's only a matter of time before she walks through that door, and I somehow have to pretend I don't want to rip her clothes off and lick every inch of her delicate skin right here on the table. I'm going to need a lot of willpower to pretend I don't want to do that.

"Do I want to know?" I peer over the rim of my glass.

Trey throws his hands up in the air. "High quality porn."

"Nope. Didn't want to know."

"Why do we always get some cheesy ass story line? Some hot girl comes in wearing a skimpy little outfit and oops, she fell on his dick. I'm not opposed to a little buildup. Get the motor revving a little bit before you stick it in her tailpipe."

"Do people watch porn for anything but the sex?" I ask.

"I don't know, man. Maybe I'm in a dry spell. It's been…" Trey's gaze wanders toward the ceiling while he concentrates and starts counting on his fingers before he looks back to me. "Fourteen days."

"That took entirely too long for you to figure out two weeks."

"I'm telling you, not having a regular release is fucking with my head. And the lack of good porn isn't helping either. Maybe I'll see if I can find someone tonight." Trey twists in his seat and glances around the bar.

While Trey is searching for his next victim, I stare at the blank screen of my phone, thinking about Parisa. I know the girls had plans to come here tonight and Parisa said she would message me when she was on her way.

"What about that one?"

Trey's question pulls me from my thoughts. "Huh?"

"Dude, you're a pretty shitty wingman." Trey turns around to face me.

"That's because I didn't sign up to be your wingman. I was left with no other choice when Bennett bailed." My gaze wanders back down to my phone.

"Oh no. None of that." Trey points to me, then to my phone. "You're waiting for something. Don't tell me it's some chick. I already lost Bennett to the L word. I can't lose you too."

"Again, I didn't volunteer for this. And what's so bad

about falling in love? You can't tell me you've actually been in love."

Trey looks me square in the eyes, elbows resting on the table as he leans in. "I have. Zero stars. I don't recommend."

"Wait, how come I've never heard about it? When did this happen?"

"It was during a dark time of my life. Emotions got involved and then poof. Everything imploded." Trey leans back in his stool and rests his arm along the back of the chair next to him. "But it's all in the past. Now it's time to look to the future. Like which girl will scream my name tonight."

"Will that be in pleasure or terror? Because I'm kinda leaning toward the latter."

"Fuck off." Trey continues to glance around the bar. "Since you suck at being my wingman, I'm going up to the bar. See if any of the ladies need me to buy them a drink." Trey swallows the last gulp of his beer and slams it down onto the table. Within seconds, he's at the bar and already has a couple of girls hanging all over him. How does he do that? But also, I'm slightly terrified to know the answer.

A few moments later, a waitress stops by and replaces the empties with another full beer. A familiar peach scent wafts around me. Instantly, my cock twitches and I get a semi. I glance to my left, then right, the owner of the familiar sweet scent nowhere in sight. All I have to do is smell peaches and my dick gets hard. Great. I reach down and adjust myself in my slacks.

My phone lights up with an incoming message. When I look down, Parisa's name pops up on the screen.

PARISA

I'll be there in a few. I have a surprise for you.

SETH

I like your surprises.

PARISA

Who else is at Porter's?

SETH

Just me and Trey, but Trey is occupied at the bar.

PARISA

I'm walking in.

As soon as I read that last message, I glance up at the door. Parisa strolls in, looks my way, and our eyes connect. A smile instantly lights up her face. I rise to my feet and greet her. I lean down to give her a kiss and she sides steps me.

"Not here." Her voice is a low whisper. She takes off her coat and hangs it over the back of the chair. "Trey still at the bar?"

I glance that way and back down to Parisa. "Yeah."

"Follow me." She grabs my hand and leads me along the perimeter of the bar to avoid any run ins with Trey. Once we reach a hallway, she stops. On the left side is the men's room and on the right the women's. Parisa contemplates her choices for two seconds before she's tugging me to the left. When we reach the door, she pushes it open. She bends at the knees to peer under the stalls. double checking to make sure they're empty. When it's confirmed it's only us in here she stands and whirls around, pulling a sign out of her purse. With a muffled slap she sticks it to the outside then shuts the door and turns the lock.

"What did you put on the door?"

"An out of order sign. I figured it would buy us some extra time with no interruptions."

"That's actually… genius."

Parisa raises one shoulder before dropping it, giving me a sly smile. "But now, I never thought I would utter the words 'make this quick' when referring to sex, but make this quick."

She hops up on the counter, shifting her knee-length skirt so the hem bunches at her knees, and spreads her legs. I take that as an invitation and nestle between them. Cupping her cheeks, my thumbs caress her soft skin, and I press my lips to hers. She tilts her head to give me better access as I kiss along her jawline. I bury my face in the crook of her neck, inhaling her peach scent. Only this time, I know where the source is. My deep breath causes Parisa to shiver.

"Did you just sniff me?"

"I guess I did. I love that you smell like peaches. Except my dick gets confused sometimes. Like earlier, someone walked by with a similar smell, and I got hard."

Parisa lets out a chuckle. "So peaches make you hard?"

"Apparently," I mumble into her neck. She reaches down and wraps her fingers around my cock that's now straining against the zipper. I release a groan. "Didn't you say you had a surprise for me?"

"I did." She grabs my hand that's resting on the countertop and slowly drags it up her thigh, under her skirt, until I reach the apex of her thighs.

"Fuck. Did you come here without panties?" I drag my finger down her slit, her wetness coating my finger. Parisa nibbles on her lip and nods. Instinctively, she spreads her legs wider, giving me better access.

"I was hoping we could finish what we started earlier today."

I peer around at our surroundings. The men's bathroom at Porter's. Luckily, Jake keeps this place fairly clean. But right now, my need for Parisa outweighs the thought of having sex in a public bathroom.

"You certainly know how to tempt me past my boundaries." I push a finger inside her needy pussy. I pump once, twice, then I add a second finger. Parisa throws her head back as she rides my hand. Her sweet moans of ecstasy echo off the tile walls. I lean in, my words a whisper against her lips. "Peach, you have to be quiet, otherwise I'm going to shove my bow tie in your mouth." Her pussy grips my fingers as if my dirty words turn her on more. "I need to be inside you." I pull my fingers out and she releases a whimper from the loss. Tugging her off the counter, I turn her around and place her hands on top of the linoleum between the sinks. I grip her chin and stare into her lust filled hazel eyes in the mirror and whisper against her ear. "Now, keep your eyes here. Fixed on me. See what you do to me. How your body is made for mine."

With my hand still holding her jaw, I use my other hand to undo the button of my pants. I tug them down, along with my boxer briefs, so they rest just above my knees. Gripping my cock, I run the head up and down her slit, spreading her wetness around. Without thinking, I press the head of my cock into her opening. Her warm heat covers me, inch by glorious inch, until I'm fully seated. She wiggles her ass and presses into me, then it hits me.

"Shit. I'm not wearing a condom. I don't have a condom." I start to pull out, but she reaches around to stop me.

"I don't care. I need you so bad right now." Again, she wiggles her ass and I use that as my cue to continue. This time, when I pull out, I slam back into her. Her moans echo in the small space.

Leaning in, I whisper against her ear, "I warned you." I use my free hand and undo my constellation patterned navy bow tie. Pulling it free, I tuck it into a ball and shove it into Parisa's willing mouth. The silky fabric drapes out, one end touching her chin. "Now keep your eyes on me."

I hike her skirt up from the hem and rest it on her lower back, giving me a full view of her perfectly round ass. Pumping my hips, I look down and watch as my glistening cock slides in and out of her pussy. My fingers grip her hips, leaving small indents in her soft flesh as my thrusts become harder. Faster. Her moans are muffled by my bow tie, but if anyone is carefully listening, they can hear her screaming my name. Reaching around, I rub circles around her clit, adding pressure that matches my thrusts. Suddenly, her pussy contracts around me and I bite back a groan to keep my own release from spilling inside her. My dick feels ready to burst. When I peer into the mirror, my gaze meets hers, and that's my undoing. After one last thrust, I pull out, shooting my cum all over her creamy flesh. I continue to pump my fist until every last spurt is covering her skin. I stare down at where I've marked her. My cum drips from her ass and runs down her thigh. Lifting my head, I meet her eyes in the mirror again. I'm falling for this girl. And falling hard.

I reach up and tug my bow tie from her mouth. She takes a moment to stretch her jaw before a smile graces her lips. I lean forward and press my lips to hers.

"Let me get you cleaned up." I tuck myself back into my pants and pull them up, forgoing the button for now. Reaching for the paper towels, I pull off a few sheets, wetting one, and clean up my mess. Once I'm done, I pull her skirt back down. I turn her around so she's facing me, my chest pressing up against hers and I cup her cheeks. My lips brush against hers. "I don't know what you're doing to me, but I like it."

"Good, because I like it, too." She beams up at me. My hands drop to the counter, caging her in. She looks down at my chest and then at my still unbuttoned pants. With deft fingers she does up the button and zips up the zipper. "We better get back out there before anyone notices."

She whirls around and uses the mirror to adjust her outfit and straighten the silver clip in her hair. In the meantime, I pull up the collar of my shirt and tie my bow tie.

Once we're situated, Parisa exits the bathroom first. She tugs her sign off the door and shoves it into her oversized purse. I wait a few minutes then leave after her. When I peer around the open bar, I notice the crowd has become larger. Instantly, like a beacon, I spot Parisa at the bar talking to another girl. I notice our table is empty, so I assume Trey is out trying to convince a girl to go home with him.

As soon as I pull out a chair and sit, Trey comes ambling up to the table.

"This place is a bust." Trey huffs.

"What? Couldn't find some girl to take pity on you?"

"Everyone has a boyfriend or some shit. Is something in the water where everyone suddenly starts settling down?" Trey peers down at his whisky sour, then fishes out the ice cubes and places them into an empty glass.

I watch him for a moment, trying to understand how his brain works, until I finally ask, "What are you doing?"

"They aren't getting me with the love tainted water."

Parisa strolls up to our table, looks at Trey, then at me. "What's he doing?"

"Don't ask." And without even thinking, I pull out the chair next to me.

Parisa takes a drink of her vodka limeade when Trey looks up at her, then at her drink. "I wouldn't drink that if I were you. The ice is tainted."

Parisa spits her drink back into the glass. "What are you talking about?"

"Shut up, Trey." I turn to Parisa. "Don't listen to him. Nothing's tainted. His ego can't take being turned down by every girl here."

"There has to be a reasonable explanation, and this is it." Trey finishes scooping out the last ice cube. "And to make matters worse, I went to use the bathroom and there was an out of order sign stuck to the men's room. I had to sneak into the women's bathroom and pray I didn't get shanked."

Parisa turns toward me at the same exact time I turn toward her, both of us trying to bite back our laughter.

"And if you're not careful—" Trey's eyebrows pinch together as his gaze flits between me and Parisa. "What's so funny?" When neither of us respond, Trey tips back the last of his iceless drink and sets it on the table. Olivia walks up to the table and throws herself in the empty chair next to Trey.

"I need a drink," Olivia huffs out.

"Me too. Let's get a round at the bar." Trey narrows his eyes at me and then his gaze drifts to Parisa, who's still trying to control her laughter. It's like a light bulb goes off behind his eyes as they widen, then his gaze meets mine. He studies me as he talks to Olivia.

Trey rises to his feet and sluggishly, Olivia follows him. "Fine, but you're buying."

"I hope you don't like ice." Trey's voice waning as they disappear into the crowd.

Fuck. Trey knows.

chapter thirteen
Organized Chaos

Parisa

"So, this is where you live?" Seth's gaze wanders around the three-story brick building as he shifts his SUV into park alongside the curb. My apartment isn't in the fanciest part of town, but it's on a quiet street and the rent is cheaper than most one-bedroom apartments in the area. This morning Seth sent me a message saying he wanted to take me out for breakfast, promising me the Bear Creek Cafe has the best french toast in town. Let me say, they did not disappoint with the cranberry and wild rice french toast with warm oatmeal stout beer syrup. That might be my new favorite breakfast place.

I open the car door and step out, the brown grass and fallen leaves crunching under my shoes. Seth rounds the hood and meets me with an outstretched hand. I gaze down at his open palm before meeting his eyes.

"You do know it's only a few steps up to the door, right?"

"I know, but I'll take every opportunity I can to touch you."

A smile skirts my lips as I place my hand into his. When our fingers intertwine, he gently squeezes my hand. I can't remember the last time someone just wanted to hold my hand, especially for only a few feet. We stroll up the short sidewalk side by side and climb the few steps before I have to release his hand to dig into my purse for my keys. Once inside, there is a long narrow hallway in front of us and a set of stairs to the left.

"Well, as you can see, this place is about three times as old as I am, so there's no elevator and I'm on the third floor."

"A little cardio never hurt anyone." Seth gestures for me to lead the way. We climb the worn brown carpeted flight of stairs and once on the landing, we continue to the second flight.

"So, is this why you have such a great ass?"

"Are you staring at my ass while we climb the stairs?"

"Like I said, it's a great ass."

All I can do is shake my head and bite back the smile that takes over my face. Once we reach the third floor, I stop at the first of the two doors. I pause to think back to what state my apartment was in before I left for breakfast with Seth this morning.

"Is something wrong?" Seth stands next to me.

"Can you just wait here for a moment while I check something inside really quick?" I nervously sink my teeth into my bottom lip, unsure if he knows why I want him to wait or not.

His brows crinkle together. "Uh. Sure."

"I'll be just a minute. I promise." I shove my key into the lock and at the sound of the click, I twist the knob and open the door just enough to squeeze my body through before shutting it behind me. My gaze wanders around my nine hundred square feet open concept apartment and, sure enough, it's still in the same disarray I left it in. Damn. Why can't I have little mice come clean my house while I'm away? I toss my purse onto a dining room chair to my right and scramble to collect my bras and panties that I left drying on my living room couch. Then I crumple everything into a ball and make a mad dash to my bedroom and throw them into the closet. I'll sort that out later.

On my way out, I grab the door handle and close it behind me. Next stop, the bathroom. I pull open my vanity drawer and do an arm sweep of all my make-up and hair products into the drawer and slam it shut. When I'm finished in the bathroom, I dash to the kitchen. I have a dishwasher… that I should use more often. Grabbing a cookie sheet, I stack all the dirty dishes on top. I scan the kitchen wondering where I can put it. Bingo. Oven. Reaching for the black handle, I yank down and shove the overflowing cookie sheet inside and slam the door shut causing the insides to rattle. Once it's quiet again, I rest a hand on the laminate countertop while I use the back of my other to wipe the sweat from my brow.

Just then a soft knock sounds in the small entryway, followed by Seth's voice. "Is everything okay in there?"

Shit. Seth. I hurry back toward the door and pause to straighten my skirt in the mirror hanging on the wall. Opening the door, I prop myself against the wood frame as Seth eyes me skeptically.

"Hi." The word is a soft whisper.

"Hi." Seth tilts his head as a smile pulls at his lips. "I heard a loud bang. Is everything alright?"

"Oh. Yes. Everything is good."

"That's good. You going to let me in?"

"Oh. Yes." I step out of the way to give Seth enough room to walk in and then I softly close the door behind him and turn the lock. Seth does a slow scan starting with my living room on the left, down a short narrow hallway, and then to my kitchen on the right. Finally, his gaze wanders back to meet mine.

"You have a nice place."

"Thanks. I would give you the tour, but this is about it." I wave my hand around the small area.

"It's cozy. I like it." Seth toes off his shoes, neatly placing them next to each other, and walks into the living room. I trail a few steps behind when I catch sight of a black lace thong camouflaged against a black buffalo plaid blanket. Quickly, I snatch it from the back of the couch before he can see. My sudden movements cause Seth to turn toward me. I flash him a dazzling smile and when he turns back around, I shove the lace fabric into the couch behind a throw pillow.

"Wow. Did you take these pictures?" Seth stops in front of several framed photographs that hang on the wall between two large windows.

"I did." My arm brushes up against his as I stand next to him. Seth looks down at me, then back at the photos.

"These are really good. You have a great eye for composition."

"Thanks. This one," I point to a black framed picture at the top, "was taken right after a storm had rolled through. I thought the clouds looked ominous over the lake, but the way the sun was peeking through the clouds made them look beautiful."

"Stunning actually." When I turn to Seth, hooded emerald eyes stare back at me. The look he's giving me makes me want to rip off his shirt and straddle his face right here in my living room, but I refrain. *Have a little self control, Parisa.*

"I took this one at one of my favorite spots." I point to a picture of a gazebo that sits along the shore of Lake Superior as the sun peeks over the horizon. Yellows and oranges paint the early morning sky.

"I know the place. It's at the end of a trail on Bristol Beach, right?"

"That's the spot. It's so quiet and peaceful, especially in the morning. Sometimes with the fog rolling in during the summer, it looks pretty too. This one has to be one of my favorites, though. I've lived here all my life and I will forever be in awe of the sea smoke over the lake. The giant wall looks very apocalyptic with the way it billows above the lake as pinks and oranges blaze behind from the rising sun. It was so cold out that morning, but getting this shot was worth it."

"You're immensely talented. Have you ever thought of entering these photos in any local contests? I'm sure these would win every award."

"Not really." I shrug my shoulder. "It's just a hobby. Helps me relax when things get stressful."

"Well, maybe you could take the photos for the new marketing campaign."

Taking a few steps back, I flop down on the couch. "It's a possibility."

The couch dips as Seth sits next to me. My legs slide toward his until our thighs touch, the contact causing my heart rate to accelerate. How can the simplest touch set me on fire? When Seth's gaze meets mine, the same desire pools behind his eyes. Feeling exhilarated, I twist to push him back against the couch and hike a leg over his lap, so I'm straddling his thighs. I cup his cheeks and press a kiss to his lips. His hands reach around me, his fingers press into my cotton covered backside to pull me closer. Goosebumps prickle my skin just from his touch. A moan escapes me, and Seth takes that as an invitation to deepen the kiss.

Before I know it, he's twisting us so that my back is on the cushions with his body hovering over me, resting most of his weight on one elbow. Seth trails his finger down my cheek, across the hollow of my neck, over my collarbone, and down my arm before he clasps my wrist and drags it over my head. Then he continues the movement on the opposite side and drags my other arm over my head. He uses one hand to clasp my wrists together, causing me to push out my chest. His gaze wanders down to where my breasts strain against the buttons of my blouse, then his lips are on mine. I wither beneath him when my fingertips graze a familiar lace fabric. While I deepen the kiss, I attempt to shove the lace farther into the couch. Shimmying under Seth, I hope he thinks I'm trying to rub against him and not hide my panties.

Seth's lips pull away from mine. "What are you doing?"

Shit. Guess I wasn't as inconspicuous as I was hoping. "Nothing." I try to feign innocence, but Seth's not buying it. How is he so observant?

He narrows his eyes at me. Then his gaze drifts up to where my hands are. He sits up, resting his weight on his elbow while he uses his other hand to toss the pillow to the floor exposing my hands.

"You're up to something." A smile spreads across his face and I can't fight the smile on mine. He pulls up on my hands and as they raise, my lace panties also comes with them. "Well, what do we have here?" Seth plucks the lace from my fingers. "Please tell me these are yours?"

A laugh escapes me. "Of course, they're mine."

"That's not like an emergency underwear supply? Like you're sitting on your couch thinking of me and then suddenly you need to change."

I slap his chest. "Oh my God! No! Who would have a secret stash of underwear in their couch?"

"I don't know. You tell me." He quirks an eyebrow.

"I did laundry earlier and set out all my bras and panties to air dry. I tried to clean up and missed a pair."

"So that's what you were doing while you made me wait in the hallway."

I cover my face with my hands, mostly to hide my embarrassment. "You are so neat and organized. I didn't want you thinking I'm a slob who doesn't know how to clean."

Seth slowly peels my hands from my face. "I'll let you in on a secret. I'm not attracted to you because of your tidiness or lack thereof. Plus, I've seen your desk at work. I know what I'm getting myself into." He winks and kisses the tip of my nose before sitting up. "I'm going to get some water. Want anything?" Seth rises to his feet and moves into the kitchen.

"I'm fine. There's bottled water in the fridge." I sit up, my butt on the edge of the cushion.

"So, the loud banging I heard while you made me wait in the hallway, that wouldn't have to do anything with you tidying up, would it?"

"Don't look in the oven." I cover my face again and flop back down on the couch.

The creak of the oven door opening echoes through the apartment. "Oh. This might be a deal breaker."

"Shut up. I didn't want you seeing them in my sink. I'm going to wash them after you leave."

Seth returns to the couch with a bottled water and sits down. He eyes me suspiciously as he twists off the cap and takes a drink. He replaces the cap and sets it down on the end table, his lips tip up into a playful grin. "Anything else you want to confess? Mystery closet filled to the ceiling?"

"No closet. But I now have a drawer in my bathroom that has all my make-up and hair products dumped inside."

"How do you live your life like this?"

"Organized chaos." I shrug my shoulders.

We sit in a comfortable silence, side by side, on the couch. But there's one question I've always been curious about and there's no time like present to find out.

Breaking the silence, I ask, "So why did you hate me so much? At work."

Seth reaches for my hand and brushes his thumb over the top. "It wasn't so much that I hated you. I just hated your disorganization. I think you're better than that. But let me ask you the same thing. Why did you hate me?"

"This is going to sound stupid. But you're so organized and put together. On the best of days, I feel like a hot mess. You make me feel inferior and I hate that."

"I'll be honest. My incessant need to be organized can drive me crazy. But I think it's more of a control thing."

"Where did it come from?"

"I can't pinpoint one specific event. It was something I grew up with and it carried into adulthood."

"So, tying me up with your bow ties is a control thing?"

Seth takes a moment to think over his answer. "I think it's a part of it. But also, it's like a release of the control."

"Well, there's definitely a release of something." I giggle and rest my head on his shoulder. Being tied up during sex is something I've never experienced, but it's something I'm growing to love, especially with Seth. Deep down, I trust him. And that thought terrifies me.

Seth squeezes my hand to get my attention and then looks down at me. "What do you say we get out of here? I want to show you something."

chapter fourteen
A Piece Of Me

Seth

"Where are we going?" She looks up at me.

"I just want to show you a part of me that not many people know about." My gaze drifts down her body before looking back up. "Well, first you might need to change. Something more casual, perhaps."

Her eyebrows squish together. "Well, that's not ominous or anything. Is this a public place?"

"Yes, but no one will recognize you. Just trust me." I press my lips to her forehead before standing and taking her with me. Spinning her around, I point her in the direction of the hallway, where I assume her bedroom is. "Now go change."

A few minutes later, she's walking down the hallway and into the living room. Parisa in a skirt and blouse…

gorgeous. Parisa in skinny jeans and flowy top… fucking stunning.

"Will this do?"

Tugging her toward me, I wrap my arms around her waist. "You look perfect. In fact, I'm not sure I want to leave your apartment anymore."

She pushes me away with a giggle. "Well, you made me change so whatever you had planned, we're going."

"Okay. Fair enough. But afterward you're mine."

"I won't argue with that."

"One more thing. Do you have a hair tie?"

"Is this another kink you have? You going to put my hair in a braid or something?"

I can't help but laugh. "No. But you'll need it."

The drive is relatively quiet. I'm kind of surprised Parisa hasn't tried to play twenty questions about where we're going. A smile tugs at my lips knowing that she trusts me. We drive down a side street before entering a dark alley. The headlights of my car light up a brick wall in front of us. I pull into a spot between two other vehicles, shift into park, and turn off the ignition.

"Dark alley. Big brick building. Either this is a secret meeting spot for an underground rave or you're going to chop me up into little bits in the basement."

"Lucky for you… neither. But we'll be chopping things. We better get going." I open my door and step out. Parisa hesitates for a moment before getting out herself. As she rounds the hood of my car I'm waiting for her, holding out my open palm. She looks down before resting her delicate hand in mine. I give her hand a squeeze; her gaze meets mine as a smile tugs at both our lips. Just one look, one touch from her, makes me want to tell the world she's mine. But she's not mine. Not yet anyway.

It's only a few steps before we're in front of a large steel door. Gripping the handle, I yank it up, holding it open for Parisa. This gives me a moment to admire her from behind. Once I close the door behind us, I give her my hand again and lead us down a dimly lit hallway as one of the fluorescent lights flickers above us, lighting our path down the well-worn, pale yellow tile. I make a mental note to get the light fixed.

"I've never known a guy who's enjoyed holding hands so much."

I lean down and whisper in her ear. "I like touching you." Even in the dim hallway I can see the blush creep up her cheeks.

Once she collects herself, she asks again, "Where are you taking me?"

"You'll see."

chapter fifteen
Fingers In My Cookie Jar

Parisa

Everything tells me I should turn around and run out of this place, but a part of me trusts Seth. Okay, a huge part. Otherwise, I wouldn't still be here, hand gripping his, and I wouldn't let him tie me up with his bow ties.

As we continue down the hallway, the murmur of voices becomes louder and louder. Once we reach the end, we turn left through a narrow doorway and a loud clatter echoes around us. It takes a moment for my eyes to adjust to the bright overhead florescent lights. I take in the small commercial kitchen, if you could even call it that. All the appliances look as if they're at least twenty years old. The pale yellow tile is either purposely that color or has discolored over the years.

"Seth, what are you doing here? It isn't Wednesday."

An older woman with salt and pepper hair greets Seth with a hug, then her gaze drifts to me. "And who is this?"

Seth smiles at her. "Maggie, this is my friend Parisa. Parisa, this is Maggie. She's the one who keeps this place from crumbling to the ground."

"You give me too much credit," Maggie says and then turns to me. "I've been working with Seth's parents since they started The Lilith House." Her attention shifts back to Seth. "So, what brings you two here?"

"We're here to help. I know it's not my usual night, but I'm sure you can find a place for us."

"Well, you know we can always use the help."

"How about me and Parisa work the line? That way, you and Wade can get a head start on tomorrow's prep and dishes."

"That's a wonderful idea. You know where to find the aprons."

Seth rests his hand on my lower back and directs me to the far corner of the kitchen where a collection of aprons hangs on a rack. He plucks one off for me and places the loop over my head. I secure the ties around my back as Seth grabs an apron for himself. He then opens a drawer and pulls something out.

"Uh, what's that?" I point to whatever he's holding.

"These sexy things are called hairnets. See why you needed a hair tie. Makes wearing one of these much easier." Seth stretches the elastic to fit over the top of my head. I finish tucking in all the loose strands. In the meantime, he does the same for himself.

"With the apron and hairnet, I don't know how I'm going to keep my hands off you." I step into his space and trail my fingertips down his chest.

Seth grabs my wrist to halt my movement as his eyes narrow into slits. "Don't start something you can't finish."

"I never do." I flash him a devious smile.

Seth tilts his head to look at the ceiling, his nostrils flare with a few deep breaths before his gaze meets mine. "You really like to test my patience. But we're here to serve others dinner." He leans down, his hot breath tickling the shell of my ear. "But later, I'll have you for dessert."

My cheeks heat and I bite my lip at the thought. The simplest words out of his mouth have a way of igniting the butterflies in my stomach. I've dated plenty of guys, but none of them have made me feel like this. He's always finding a way to touch me, telling me all the things he wants to do to me because if he doesn't get them out, he might not do them. And that thought has me clenching my thighs together. But wait… are we dating? Before I can think on this too much, Seth interrupts my thoughts.

"They already have most of the food out, but take these utensils and follow me." Seth bends down and places a chaste kiss on my lips and gives me a handful of metal spoons and tongs. Then he exits through a door off to the side and I pick up my pace before he can get too far.

After the buffet trays are set up on top of the banquet tables, I stand next to Seth. He's serving turkey and ham while I'm in charge of peas and potatoes.

The makeshift dinner area is about half the size of a gymnasium. Worn cafeteria style tables form rows throughout the room, leaving just enough space to walk between them. A line of hungry guests starts to form in the hallway just outside the cafeteria. I wipe my palms on my apron, unsure why my nerves are getting the best of me. I'm just serving food to a bunch of hungry people. But this is something that's so important to Seth, and I don't want to mess up.

Once the line is allowed to enter, I instantly put a friendly smile on my face. But after I see the way Seth interacts with everyone as if they are old friends, I no longer need to fake my smile. Even though everyone here may not be able to afford a warm meal, Seth treats them all as if they're just regular people. No judgment. And that makes me fall for him even more.

"Parisa, this is Mr. Rickett. You gotta watch out for him. He'll try to sweet talk you into getting extra potatoes." Seth points his tongs at Mr. Rickett as a smile tugs at his lips.

"Hey now, you can't be giving away all my secrets," Mr. Rickett says to Seth before bringing his attention to me. "You can call me Lenard. So, what's such a pretty lady doing hanging out with this one?" He hikes his thumb toward Seth.

"I can't hang out with pretty ladies?" Seth asks.

"Well, I've never seen you bring any around here before."

"Fair enough, Lenard."

"You can still call me Mr. Rickett. Only the pretty girls can call me Lenard."

"Ah, I see how it is. We still on for a game of Euchre on Wednesday?"

"Of course. Can't let you break my winning streak."

Seth turns to me. "I swear he hides cards up his sleeve or something. Every time, he always manages to come back and beat me."

A wide grin covers my cheeks as I listen to these two banter back and forth. "Well Lenard, since you're able to bring this one," I hike my thumb toward Seth, "down a peg or two, I'll happily give you an extra scoop of potatoes."

"See, I knew I liked you. You better keep her around." Lenard gives Seth a stern look.

Seth smiles. "That's just because she caved and gave you extra potatoes."

Lenard moves down the line to the next server, his smile bright but not as bright as it was while he was talking to Seth.

"Watch this," Seth leans down to whisper in my ear, "he'll grab two cookies and put one in his pocket."

Sure enough, Lenard takes two cookies and deposits one into the pocket of his light flannel jacket.

I turn to Seth. "How did you know?"

"He's been doing that since the first day he came here. It's not hurting anything, so we just let it slide. Plus, he likes to share with a little boy who comes in here with his mom."

My gaze lingers on Lenard a little longer. I can't imagine being in a position where my only meal for the day would come from a community kitchen.

Once we finish serving the last person in line, we begin cleaning up. Seth grabs the buffet trays and I take the utensils and go into the kitchen so Maggie and Wade can wrap up any of the leftover food and start washing the dishes. When the serving area is wiped down, we start on the dining area. Some people are still scattered at a few of the tables so we work around them. Finally, when the dining room is empty, I lean against one table as Seth passes me a bottle of water.

"I'll be honest. I never expected this to be so much work." I twist off the cap and swallow down a big gulp.

"It is. But just imagine if people weren't here to help, all those people wouldn't get a hot meal for the evening."

"Yeah. I'm really glad you brought me here."

Seth stares off to the far wall, deep in thought, before he speaks. "This place means a lot to my parents. To me as well. It's a small thing I can do to make the world better. I just wish we could do more. But with the limited space and dilapidated equipment, we're doing the best we can."

I place my water bottle on the table and move to stand in front of Seth. Raising my hands, I gently cup his cheeks and gaze into his green eyes. "You are doing amazing things here. Don't doubt that for one second." His day-old stubble tickles my fingertips. I stretch up on my tippy toes and place a chaste kiss on his lips. His hands go to my hips and pull me closer.

"Seth! I need you!" Maggie yells from the kitchen.

Immediately, we both run to the kitchen. As soon as we're through the doorway, all we see is water gushing out the side of the commercial dishwasher. A puddle of suds and water collects on the floor. Seth rushes over, his shoes splashing in the puddle as he bends down to shut off the main water supply to the dishwasher. My gaze is glued to the way his forearm muscles flex with each turn. When did forearms get so sexy? When Seth stands up, he looks around at the damage before exhaling a deep sigh.

"Seth, I'm so sorry. I hit start and everything was working fine and then suddenly water just started shooting everywhere. I pressed the stop button, but it wasn't working." Panic laces Maggie's voice.

"That's okay. It's not your fault. The washer has given us some troubles before. Now I guess today was its last."

"What happened in here? I leave you alone for five minutes and you flood the place." Wade laughs and wraps his arm around Maggie's shoulder. "Well, I'm glad to see it's not just our house where she breaks things."

Maggie softly slaps his chest as she leans into him. "It's the only way I get new things."

"The dishwasher needed replacing a long time ago. You can only put a Band-Aid on a bullet wound for so long," Seth says.

"I'll grab a couple of mops and we'll get this cleaned up." Wade turns and heads to the utility closet.

Once the floor is dry, Seth tells Wade and Maggie to go home since they have to be back tomorrow, and we'll finish the dishes. I'm standing in front of the deep well stainless sink spraying the soap off the pans as Seth passes them to me. We work together effortlessly. Maybe we should have tried working together like this sooner. I bet we would have been way more productive instead of working against each other. A smile forms on my lips.

"What's that smile for?" Seth tilts his head, looking at me.

"Oh, just thinking about how we actually make a good team and probably would have been more productive if we hadn't been trying to sabotage each other."

"I never tried to sabotage you."

"Hiding my papers and making me late for meetings wasn't sabotage?"

"Just teaching you a lesson on organization." Seth winks at me.

"You're such an ass." I point the sprayer in his direction and squeeze the handle, sending a spray of water toward Seth. He jumps back, but not before the water hits his chest. I release a giggle.

Seth's nostrils flare and he narrows his eyes at me. Before I know it, his hand dips into the sink and he scoops up a pile of soap suds and throws it in my direction. I let out a squeal as the suds splatter on my face. Wiping the soap from my eyes, Seth's smiling triumphantly at me.

This. Is. War.

I scoop up a handful of suds and throw it back at him. My aim not as good as his, only half hits him on the cheek and the rest falls to his shoulder. I reach into the sink for another handful of suds but Seth's arms around wrap around my waist and tugs, so my back is against his chest. He spins me around with his hands on my hips, then he lifts and plops me up on a steel table and stands between my open legs.

"Always a pain in my ass. This is why I always need to tie you up, so you keep your hands to yourself."

"Unlucky for me, you're not wearing a bow tie today."

"I'm a resourceful man. I'm sure I could find something to use."

I thread my fingers through his hair before tugging him toward me and then crash my lips to his. I don't know what I enjoy more, annoying him or kissing him. Both are equally enjoyable.

His hands trail up my thighs, causing goosebumps to sprout along my skin. His tongue presses at the seam of my lips, and I open to let him in. I caress my tongue against his as this slow waltz between us turns into something closer to dirty dancing.

"Oh! I'm so sorry."

Immediately, we pull away like we've been caught with a hand in the cookie jar. I'm sure if it weren't for this interruption, Seth's fingers would have been in *my* cookie jar. Seth straightens his shirt and I hop off the counter as we both peer at Maggie, who has her hand covering her eyes while she blindly tries to navigate through the kitchen.

"I just forgot to grab my jacket. I'll be out of your way in just a second and you can continue what you were doing," Maggie rushes out.

"It's okay, Maggie. You can open your eyes. I don't want you hurting yourself," Seth says.

Maggie parts her fingers as she peeks out to make sure the coast is clear before dropping her hand. She spots her jacket and dashes to pluck it off the counter. "Got it. I'll let you two get back to it." She gives us both a sly smile before she turns to me. "So lovely to meet you, Parisa. I hope to see you around more often." Her hand lingers on my forearm as I return her smile and then she's out the door.

"That was a close one." I slump back to lean on the counter. So much for keeping this a secret.

"Maggie won't say anything. Now, if it had been my mom, we might have a little more explaining to do." Seth moves to stand in front of me, his hands rest on the counter, caging me in.

"Exactly. What if that had been your mom?"

"But it wasn't. Plus, would it be that big a deal if someone else found out?"

"It's just something I'm not ready for. Let's finish cleaning and you can bring me home, okay?" My tone is harsher than I wanted.

Seth nods in agreement and pushes off the counter. We finish cleaning up the kitchen in awkward silence.

chapter sixteen
You're Not Parisa

Seth

I pull into a parking spot outside the small grocery store on the opposite side of town. Sure, I could go to the bigger chain store, but I prefer supporting the smaller family run stores. But the real reason is this one's closer to Parisa's apartment and I secretly hope I run into her and can make her talk to me. All week Parisa's given me the cold shoulder and I don't know what I said or did to make her so frightened. No stolen glances while we work, no not so random run ins in our secret hallway for a passing kiss. Nothing. She just puts her head down and pretends I don't exist. It's like she's embarrassed to be with me or something. But I quickly shake that thought out of my head as I exit my car.

Once inside, I grab a cart and pull up my notes app to

see what I have on my list, but a wave of familiar auburn hair catches my attention. I quicken my pace to follow her down aisle three. As I round the endcap, I almost take out an elderly lady reaching for a box of Wheaties. I give her a sheepish smile and apologize as I pass before I continue my way down the aisle.

"Parisa!" I call out her name, but she keeps walking until she rounds the corner. I jog down the aisle, following her. I spot her a few aisles down and I yell again, but it's like she's ignoring me. Finally, she stops in front of a shelf of cereal boxes and that gives me enough time to catch up to her. "Parisa!" With her back to me, her head is down while she reads the back of a box. I reach out and grab her shoulder. She twists around with a shriek and throws the box at my chest. Quickly, I catch it before it falls to the floor. That's when recognition hits me. This isn't Parisa. Same hair, same piercing hazel eyes, but Parisa doesn't have a scar on her chin.

"You're not Parisa," I say as I step back so I'm a good arm's length away in case she tries to throw another box at me.

She pulls her ear buds from her ears and tilts her head at me. "Do I know you?"

"Oh, sorry, you just look eerily familiar. Do you know Parisa Anthony?"

Recognition hits her face. "Oh, are you Seth?"

"Yes. But how do you know me?"

"Parisa. That's my sister. Twin sister to be exact. She's mentioned a Seth who likes to wear colorful bow ties and black rimmed glasses." She points to my navy blue plaid bow tie. "I'm Hollyn." She holds out her hand for me to shake.

"So, she's talked about me?"

She chuckles. "Don't flatter yourself. I wouldn't exactly

say they were good things. Just how annoying you are with the nitpicking and how everything needs to be so precise and organized—"

"Thanks, I got it. But she hasn't said anything else, maybe more recently?" My eyebrows raise in anticipation that maybe she's mentioned me to someone.

She taps her chin for a moment. "Come to think of it, she hasn't mentioned anything about you in a while. Maybe you haven't got on her last nerve as of late? She has been cheerier and more upbeat lately. Did you quit?"

Supplying her with plenty of orgasms is what I want to say, but think better of it. "No, we still work together. Well currently, she's not speaking to me and I'm not sure why. We've been able to bond over a mutual interest the last few weeks so things have been good, but I must have said something to make her mad."

"I know she's had some issues with previous co-workers. It's not really my place to tell, so you'll have to ask her. Sorry I can't be more of a help."

"No. That's alright. You've helped a lot. Also, what's with the ear buds in the grocery store? It's not very safe. Anyone could sneak up on you. Like I just did."

"It's helps me stay focused. Have you ever gone grocery shopping on an empty stomach?"

"No." I give her a slight headshake.

"Don't. Otherwise, you end up with a cart full of junk and nothing you came here for."

"Noted. But what if something were to happen? How would you know?"

"If you were about to be hit by a bus, would you rather know it's coming or would you rather have it just happen?"

"I would want to know so I can plan and prepare."

"And I would rather leave it a surprise."

I nod at her response.

"But I should get going. It was nice to finally meet you, Seth." She turns around and continues her way down the aisle, but quickly twirls around. "Also…" Her voice causes me to lift my head. "If you didn't know, her favorite flowers are dahlias. Just don't tell her I told you. And stop by my bakery, The Sweet Spot. If you're armed with her favorite treat, a chocolate salted caramel cupcake, she won't be able to resist you." She digs in her wrist wallet and passes me her business card before giving me a wink.

Then she's turning around again, but I call out to her, and she spins around. "Can you not say anything to Parisa?" She motions as if she's zipping her lips, then she's out of sight. I stare down at the white card stock with The Sweet Spot in raised ink on the top. Flowers and cupcakes. Sounds easy enough, but a gut feeling tells me it's not going to be that easy.

chapter seventeen
You'll Find Me Waiting

Parisa

A soft knock on my door startles me from watching reruns on the television. Maybe that's what I need to do. Move to a small town and fall in love with my neighbor, but maybe skip the whole hating each other thing because I'm so over that. Then the knock sounds again, slightly more aggressive this time, and I jump to my feet. Before answering, I gaze through the peephole, but only an arrangement of light and dark pink dahlias fill the glass hole.

Upon opening the door, a teenage boy with long, floppy hair whirls around and shoves the bouquet at me. "Who are these from? How did you get in here?" I spit out the questions because I don't know what else to say.

The kid shoves his hand through his hair to push it out

of his face. "Some guy paid me twenty bucks to bring these up here after he got one of your neighbors to open the front door."

I grab the vase from him and before I can say thank you, he's descending the stairs. Turning around, I kick the door closed with my foot and make my way into the kitchen to set the flowers down. Bending at the waist, I inhale their light floral scent. Delicately placed inside the bouquet, I find a card and pull it out. Dragging my finger across the back to break the seal, I pull out a small white card. Turning it over, I read what's written.

Peach,

I'm sorry I spooked you earlier. That was never my intention. If I'm being perfectly honest, I feel like I'm free falling off a cliff for you. And I want to tell you in person. So, head out to your car and you'll find your next clue.

Seth

A smile instantly tugs at my lips. As much as this man drives me crazy, it's the best kind of crazy. I don't know what got into me after Maggie caught us kissing. This arrangement was supposed to be just between the two of us because once other people find out that's when people talk. And I don't want people talking. But I can stop fooling myself, he's constantly on my mind. It's more than the orgasms, even though those are nice too. I miss talking to him and his random tidbits of knowledge. If he can go to this length for me, the least I can do is give him an explanation for my behavior.

Tugging the cardigan off my chair in the dining room, I throw it on while I shove my feet into my shoes. I look down at my ridiculous outfit of yoga pants, tank top, and oversized cardigan and realize I don't care what I look like, and I know Seth won't either. Then I'm out the door. Once I reach the back parking lot, I stop dead in my tracks. Tucked into the door handle of my black SUV is another pink dahlia and another note. Jogging to my car, my heart pitter patters in my chest as I open the folded piece of paper.

> Peach,
> Head to Bristol Beach. Inside the Free Little Library is a copy of your favorite book and there you will find your next clue.
> Seth

With my pulse racing and a wide grin taking over my face, I throw open my car door and turn over the ignition. I've never had a guy do something so sweet and romantic for me and he's not even my boyfriend. Then I think of the ex and my heart sinks a little. But Seth isn't like him, right?

Pulling out of the apartment parking lot, I turn right and drive toward the lake. There are five stop lights from my place to the park where Bristol Beach is located, and I've managed to hit every red light.

By the time I finally pull into the park, anticipation is buzzing through my body. I find the closest empty parking spot and pull in. Luckily, now that the weather is getting cooler, not as many people like to enjoy the beach, except for the few dedicated people who delight in watching the transformation of the green leaves to orange, red, and yellow as they walk the trails.

As soon as I spot the Free Little Library, I jog over to it with hopes I have no issue finding the book because even though I've pushed Seth away all week, I've missed him so much. And I have no idea how I want to navigate this, but I want to figure it out with him. Once I find the wood box, I pinpoint the book that I know must be for me through the glass door. Unhooking the latch, I open the door and pull out the book. *Dear Life* by Meghan Quinn. I run my finger down the cover. I can't believe he remembered. Out of hours of conversation we've had, he remembered this. Flipping open the cover, I'm greeted with another note. Tucking the book under my arm, I peel back the layers of folded paper until I see his handwriting.

> *Peach,*
> *Follow the path next to the picnic area*
> *and you'll find me waiting in the gazebo.*
> *Seth*

My heart rate spikes as I know the exact spot where he's waiting. I've been there many times to take photographs. Hurriedly, I find the pebbled pathway and follow the trail through the trees. With each step, the fallen leaves crunch beneath my feet. Between a pair of pine trees, the gazebo comes into sight, and I pick up my pace.

Finally, when I reach the opening, I slow my strides. Sitting on top of a picnic table inside the gazebo along the shoreline is Seth, as he looks out toward the horizon over the lake. Where water meets the sky. The vast openness of possibilities. That's when I realize I don't want to fight my feelings anymore.

I try to sneak up on him, but the rustle of leaves gives me away and he turns around, a beaming smile taking over his face. I can't help but reciprocate with a smile of my own. Seth climbs down to his feet and greets me with his arms wrapping around my waist, almost swallowing me whole. I bury my head in his chest and inhale his scent I'm so familiar with.

With his chin resting on top of my head, he breaks the

silence. "I'm glad you were able to follow the clues to find me."

"This is the sweetest thing anyone has ever done for me. And the book, I love it. How did you know no one was going to take it?" I clutch the book to my chest.

"I didn't. I took a chance and held out hope. And I prayed you would actually follow directions for once." The corners of his eyes crinkle as his lips pull into a smile.

"Very funny. I know how to follow directions." I elbow him in the ribs.

"The only time you're good at following directions is when an orgasm is soon to follow."

"See. You know exactly how to get me to listen."

"Here, let's sit." Seth guides me to the front of a picnic table, and we take a seat on the top as our feet rest on the bench. "Are you cold? I have a blanket. Also, I brought some hot chocolate." Seth holds up a red thermos.

"Hot chocolate sounds amazing, actually."

Seth pulls out two mugs from the bag he brought with him and fills both our cups.

"Marshmallows?" He holds up a bag of tiny marshmallows.

"Always. Who drinks hot chocolate without marshmallows?"

"My thoughts exactly." Seth plops a scoop of marshmallows into my steaming cup of hot chocolate and passes it to me.

I bring the metal camp mug up to my nose with both hands, the warmth radiating to my fingers, and inhale a deep breath. The aroma of sweet, chocolaty liquid mixed with the sweet marshmallow warms my soul. I take a sip. It tastes even better than it smells. I take another sip before I set my mug down and when I turn toward Seth, he's holding out a cupcake.

"I was told the way to your heart was with your favorite cupcake." Sitting in the palm of Seth's outstretched hand is a chocolate salted caramel cupcake.

"How did you know?" I pluck the fluffy frosted cake from his hand and peel back the wrapper with The Sweet Spot logo printed on the side and take a bite.

"I ran into your sister at the grocery store. I didn't realize you had a twin. Could have made things less awkward when she assaulted me with a cereal box."

Little bits of cake fly out of my mouth as I cough at his response. Seth reaches around and hands me my hot chocolate for a drink. Once my coughing fit is over, I respond. "That must be why she was always smiling at me whenever I saw her."

"I asked her not to say anything."

I take another bite of my cupcake, buying myself extra time to decide on what I want to say to him. Since there are no perfect words, I just let it out. "I owe you an explanation."

"For what?" Seth turns toward me.

"For everything. My behavior. Why I want to keep this between us." He says nothing, so I continue. "At my last job, I started dating a co-worker."

Seth raises an eyebrow and I huff out a laugh.

"I know, me and co-workers. Anyway, we didn't tell anyone we were seeing each other. We had different positions, but I worked a level above him. One day, I saw they were hiring for a marketing manager, and I figured I had been there awhile, I should apply." When I look up into his eyes, he's staring back at me. Listening to every word I have to say as if it's his lifeline. Just knowing that he cares about what I have to say encourages me to continue. "When I mentioned the new position to my boyfriend, he also told me to apply. They would be stupid not to promote me. Then later, I overheard him talking with some of his friends about how he applied for the position I told him about."

"Wow. That's a jerk move."

"It was. So, I confronted him about it. Maybe I shouldn't have done that in front of his friends, but heat of the moment and whatnot. Essentially, our relationship was over, but then I kept hearing whispers and murmurs going around the office that I was sleeping with him so he would let me have the position. Then more rumors started that I was sleeping with the boss to get the position." I look away and a sob gets lodged in my throat and my cheeks heat from embarrassment. Seth reaches for my chin, his gentle fingertips graze my heated skin and turns my head so my focus is back on him.

"Hey, look at me. You've got nothing to be embarrassed about. You did nothing wrong. He couldn't stand the idea of a woman beating him, so he needed to take some low blows to make himself feel better."

"Well, it worked. He got the job even though I was more qualified for it." I swipe away a stray tear.

Seth cups my cheeks, his warm skin against mine calms me. "You are too beautiful to be shedding tears over a guy like that." His sweet words cause another tear to fall. This time he swipes it away. "What did I say about the tears?"

"That last one was your fault." I look up at him through blurry eyes and give him a small smile. A moment later, his soft, warm lips are on mine in a tender kiss. Not full of heat and passion, but loving and adoring and I feel it all the way to my toes.

He pulls away but just barely, his lips only a millimeter from mine. "Want to get out of here?"

Wanting to stay in this little bubble for a bit longer I reply, "Can we stay a little longer?"

"Of course." He presses his lips to mine in a chaste kiss before pulling away and wrapping his arm around my shoulder and tucking me under his arm. I wrap my arms around his waist under his jacket, relishing in the warmth of his body. "I'm glad you didn't get the job."

"Why's that?"

"Then we would have never gotten this."

chapter eighteen
Looks Cooler
In The Movies

Parisa

"Everyone, raise your glass. Congratulations, Charlie!" Olivia shouts over the noise at Porter's. "Here's to your last day at The Blue Stone Group. The chair next to me will forever be empty without you."

The clinking of glasses and bottles echoes around our table along with a collective cheer.

Charlie sets her glass down. "Thanks everyone. It's going to be so weird not seeing everyone Monday morning anymore."

"I'm sure they'll give you your job back." I playfully nudge Charlie. Work won't be the same without seeing one of my best friends every day. Don't get me wrong, I'm ecstatic she's found love with a man who is worthy of her. I'm just having a moment of selfishness.

"What will you do with all your time now?" Seth asks.

Bennett wraps his arm around Charlie's waist and pulls her close. "Don't worry guys, I'll keep her busy." He winks.

"Oh yeah. I'm sure you'll keep her plenty busy." Trey wiggles his eyebrows and Olivia smacks him on the arm.

While the two guys bicker back and forth, a large palm rests on my leg just above my knee. I peer over to Seth and his lips twitch into a smile. His thumb caresses back and forth over my denim covered thigh, the small gesture sending a current of electricity through my body. Then his hand travels up my leg and he slowly drags it up the inseam until he reaches the apex of my thighs. Instantly, I clench my legs together trapping his fingers. If his hand traveled any farther north, he would find a very obvious wet spot from his touch.

"And I have these!" Charlie's outburst pulls me from my daydream. She reaches down into her bag and sets a white box imprinted with The Sweet Spot logo on the table. "This will be my last Friday cupcake day, so I had to get them." She flips open the box showcasing the salted caramel cupcakes with coconut brittle.

I peer into the box. "These aren't plain vanilla with a buttercream frosting." I eye her suspiciously.

She shrugs a shoulder. "It was time for something different. Something unpredictable." A smile graces her face as she wraps her arms around Bennett's waist. Instinctively, his arm wraps around her shoulder and he places a quick kiss on her forehead.

Their lovey-dovey moment is making me want to have one of my own with Seth in private.

Bennett swings his arm, causing Charlie's clutch to fly to the floor. When Charlie bends down to retrieve it, I nod my head to Seth, wordlessly telling him we should leave. As

I turn back toward everyone at the table, Charlie is eyeing me suspiciously. That's when I know it's time to go.

"It's been fun, everyone. I have a few things at home I need to get done so I'm going to call it a night." Both Olivia and Charlie stand, and I give them a round of hugs.

Seth rises from his seat as well. "Yeah. I'm going to head out, too. I've got some things to do."

Wanting to make it appear like we're not leaving together, I leave first. Luckily, Bennett stops Seth and that buys me a head start. Giving everyone a wave over my shoulder as I meander through the tables toward the exit, a hand on my elbow stops me.

"Hey, Parisa."

Just the sound of his voice makes me want to jab a pencil in my ear. Any bedroom playtime with Seth is now ruined since my vagina has shriveled up and gone drier than the Sahara Desert. Clenching my jaw, I turn around. "What do you want, Chet?"

"Is that all you have to say to me?"

I cross my arms over my chest. "Well, I was being polite, but since that's out the window… Go fuck yourself."

"Aww, you know it's so much better when you're there with me." He winks at his two other friends at the table.

"You're so disgusting. I'm glad we broke up. It's been the best thing that's happened to me."

"Oh, come on, you know you miss me." Chet stands so he's right in front of me and rubs his grimy hands up and down my biceps.

I shake him off and take a step back. "I miss you as much as I would miss a yeast infection."

"Hey Parisa, is everything okay?" Seth stands next to me.

"Yeah, I'm fine. Let's get out of here." Instinctively, I

grab Seth's hand and start to walk away, but Chet sidesteps into my path.

"Whoa. No need to leave so soon. This your new boyfriend? If you ask me, I'd say you downgraded." Chet sizes up Seth.

"It's a good thing no one asked you then," I say.

"Come on Parisa. We had some good times together. You always liked that thing I did with my tongue. Wanna go back to my place, and we can relive some old memories?"

"I would find more pleasure in setting myself on fire than ever being with you again," I spit back.

"And this guy knows how to keep you satisfied? Wait, let me guess, he's a co-worker of yours?"

"Keep Seth out of this."

Chet leans around me to look at Seth. "She's got a thing for co-workers. Always opening her legs to get to the top."

"Fuck off, Chet. I told you about that position. And I had more qualifications, but because you have a penis, they gave you the job instead."

Seth steps in front of me. "How about you leave her alone? She didn't do anything to you."

"Didn't do anything to me? You hear this bullshit she's spouting? Thinking she's better than me." Chet sneers at Seth.

"Because I am better than you. You're beneath me. The moment you told everyone I was sleeping with you so I could get the promotion, I knew I was better than you. Hell, Seth is way better than you are." My gaze drifts to Seth, then back to Chet. "Everyone in the bar is better than you."

"Holy shit. You two *are* fucking. And what's with the bow tie? This isn't the 1900s." Chet flicks Seth's bow tie.

I've never seen Seth so angry. I'm surprised steam isn't shooting out of his ears. He wraps an arm around my waist, guiding me so I'm behind him and steps up into Chet's face. "Don't touch me. Don't touch Parisa. Hell, don't even talk to her. She's done with you."

Chet takes a step closer until he's nose to nose with Seth. "Oh yeah, and what are you going to do if I do?"

I step out of the way as Seth shoves Chet's chest, so he's no longer in his face. He stumbles back a few steps before finding his balance. The two guys sitting with Chet stand and congregate behind him. His eyes narrow to slits before he comes after Seth with a right hook.

Acting quickly, Seth ducks out of the way and takes a step back as Chet stumbles into a table, knocking over a pint glass that shatters on the ground. The noise draws attention from the other bar patrons. When he rights himself, he flares his nostrils, and he comes after Seth. But this time Seth balls his fingers into a fist and hits him in his left cheek. Chet stumbles back again and nearly hits the floor, but his friends catch him. Bennett and Trey appear behind us ready to stick up for their friend. Chet lunges for Seth, but a muscular arm across his chest halts him in his tracks.

"Dude. What the fuck? Get off me." Chet struggles, but is no match against Jake's strength.

"I have one rule here. No fighting. And your dumbass couldn't follow that. Now you can get the fuck out or I can throw your ass out. The choice is yours."

"He started it. He punched me. You should throw his ass out."

"I know him. He's cool. Now you on the other hand, I don't know who the fuck you are, so you get to leave. Got it?" Chet struggles in the restraint so Jake tightens his grip a bit more. "Got it?"

"Fuck. Shit. Yeah. Got it. Now just let me go." Jake releases him and pushes him away in the process. "Come on, guys. Let's go. Nothing but trash here, anyway." Jake fake lunges at them. The three of them flinch and scurry away.

"Thanks Jake. Sorry about all the commotion." Seth clenches and unclenches his fist.

"Don't worry about it. You need some ice for your hand?" Jake asks.

"Yeah. That would be great."

Jake turns and heads back toward the bar.

"Oh my God Seth. Are you alright?" He flinches when I lift his hand. I run my fingers over his swollen knuckles.

"I'll be fine. They definitely make punching someone look a lot cooler in the movies." He continues to stretch out his fingers. I start to bring his hand up to kiss his knuckles like my mom would do when I was a child and I hurt myself, then it hits me where we are and who's watching and I drop his hand like it's on fire. When I look up, I'm met with sad eyes gazing back at me.

"Holy shit Rocky. I never thought we'd see the day that you would punch someone. I feel like such a proud father." Trey wraps his arms around Seth's shoulders. "Now son, next time, you need to hit him with a right hook and then a left jab. He'll be counting stars after that." Trey starts singing "Eye of the Tiger" while throwing one-handed punches into the air.

Seth shrugs Trey off him. "There won't be a next time."

Jake returns with a bag of ice and Seth grabs it to place on his swollen knuckles. He just punched a guy to defend my honor. I don't know how he does it, but right when I think I'm immune to his charm, he does something to surprise me. A guy has never stood up for me like that and I can't even show him how much I truly appreciate him.

"I gotta get back behind the bar, but the next round is on me." Jake makes his way back to the bar as another bartender comes over with a mop and broom and cleans up the mess.

"Seth, you should get into fights more often. Free drinks." Trey fist pumps the air and makes his way to the bar.

"I don't think I'll be staying. I'll need to get some fresh ice for this soon." Seth holds up his hand, then he bolts toward the exit.

"Yeah. I'm going to get going too. Too much excitement for one night for me," I say.

We do another round of goodbyes and hugs. When I look up, Seth is already out the door. Hastily, I move through the crowd of people and push open the door. Instantly, the cool air hits my heated face. Jogging down the sidewalk, I catch up with Seth at the end of the block.

"Hey Seth, wait up." He turns around and I stop a foot shy of where he's standing, disappointment etched across his face. "Thank you. For back there." I hike my thumb toward the bar. "I really appreciate you standing up for me when you didn't have to."

"No big deal, Parisa. That guy was being an asshole and no girl deserves that."

"And you punched him. For me." I reach for his hand and this time I do bring it up to my lips and place a small kiss on his knuckles that are starting to bruise. While still holding his hand, I gaze up into his eyes and all the feelings from before the fight come rushing back to me like a tidal wave. "Come back to my place?"

chapter nineteen
Scream My Name

Seth

"Come back to my place?"

Parisa looks up to me through her lashes, a lust filled sparkle in her hazel eyes, my hand still nestled in hers. I want to say no. Make her realize she can't continue to push me away and then pull me close when it's convenient for her. But I'm a glutton for punishment and I'll take her anyway I can.

"My car is right around the corner."

She tugs on my hand, and I wince from the pain as she drags me down the sidewalk. "We'll pick up mine later."

Once we're close enough, I unlock the doors with my key fob. I open the passenger side door and wait for Parisa to get in. She sits down, her feet dangling out the open door. Her fist grabs the front of my shirt and tugs me down. "Times like these a tie would be much more convenient." Her lips crash to mine in a bruising kiss. Her hands thread through the short hairs on the back of my head while I run mine up her thighs. Eventually the dome light shuts off, shrouding us in the dim glow from the streetlight. Her legs wrap around me and tug me closer, and I lose my balance, falling into her as her back hits the center console. A murmur of pain escapes Parisa.

I pull away. "You alright?"

"This might be more comfortable if we get in the back?"

"How about we just go back to your place? Plus, it's a little cold out here. Then you can scream my name as loud as you like because we all know you're a screamer."

"I am not!" She playfully pushes at my chest.

Before she can move her hand, I cover it with mine. I lean down, my breath a whisper on the shell of her ear. "I'm pretty sure your entire building knows my name."

"Well, I just got new neighbors and I don't believe they know your name yet."

"It would be very rude if you didn't introduce me to them." She sits up and buries her face into the front of my shirt, her shoulders bouncing in laughter. I bend down, placing a kiss on the top of her head, inhaling her peach scent. "Let's get out of here." Backing away, I give her space so she can slide her legs into the car. Once she's in, I close the door.

On the entire drive to her house her hands were all over me. Starting innocently with her hand on my thigh, she would drag her finger nails up and down over the fabric. Then her dainty hand would rub then squeeze. By the time

I turned onto her street, my dick was aching and straining against my zipper.

Now we're at her apartment and it's time for me to return the favor. Let's see how much she can concentrate on unlocking her door. Standing behind her, I drag my fingertips up the outside of her thighs, over her hips, until I get to her waist. With feather-light touches, my fingers dance across her torso and up the center of her chest. At the same time, I press a kiss to her shoulder, then up to her neck, and make my way to the spot behind her ear that drives her wild. I tug on her ear lobe with my teeth as her head falls back to my chest. A soft moan escapes her lips as she fumbles with her keys before they clatter to the ground.

"See? It's hard to concentrate when someone's distracting you," I whisper.

"Shut up. If we don't get on the other side of this door in five seconds, my neighbors will know more than just your name."

I place one more kiss on her neck before bending down and picking up the keys. Slowly I rise, pressing my front to her back, my obvious hard on poking her along the way. I reach around and very carefully push the key into the lock. Frustrated at my pace, Parisa places her hand over mine, twisting the key and shoving the door open, taking me with her.

Once we're through the doorway, she tosses her keys toward a small table next to the door, but they end up hitting the side and falling to the floor. Turning around she shoves me up against the closed door.

"Is this how we're going to do it?" I'm even more turned on by her assertiveness.

"It's always my way."

That's what she thinks. Bending down, I wrap my arms under her butt and instinctively her legs wrap around my waist. I walk forward a few feet and when her butt hits the table I deposit her on top while stepping between her spread legs. I snake my hands up her back until they wrap around her loose strands, lightly tugging down so she's forced to look up at me. With my fingers still wrapped in her hair I crash my lips to hers. Her hands grip my waist, pulling me forward. My tongue presses into the seam of her lips seeking entrance. Her lips part and our tongues meet in a fury of heat and passion. Stroking and caressing.

My fingers comb through her soft locks, while hers creep under my shirt and up my bare back. Then her nails drag back down, leaving a trail of heat in their wake. But then she pulls away, mumbling against my lips.

"Is your leg vibrating, or are you just happy to see me?"

"Shit." I dig into my pocket to check my phone. A text from Trey flashes across the screen. I ignore it and shove it back into my pocket and continue showering Parisa with kisses. On her cheek. Behind her ear. Down her neck. But my vibrating phone interrupts once again.

Pulling my phone from my pocket I notice a string of text messages from Trey. This time I turn my phone to silent and toss it across the table. He's done interrupting all the dirty things I'm going to do to Parisa. "Now where were we?"

"I think we were about to introduce you to my neighbors." She tugs the end of my bow tie until it's in her grasp. "We'll need this later."

She places the fabric on the table next to her then unbuttons my shirt until it hangs open. Her fingertips trail down my chest, over the small patch of hair, and down my abs. My hooded eyes watch in fascination as she takes in every inch of my bare chest. Hazel eyes peer up at me through long lashes, lust and passion pool in her irises. Reaching down, she grabs the bottom of her shirt and tugs up. The fabric slowly drags across her stomach and over her lace covered breasts. I assist her with taking it off completely, then she tosses it behind her.

Bending down, I place a kiss on the swell of her left breast, then do the same to the right. Parisa's head tilts back, lips parted, relishing in the sensation. I skim my fingertips up her rib cage until I reach her bra. I cup each breast before giving them a gentle squeeze, my thumbs brushing over each taught nipple. A moan escapes Parisa as she rubs her denim covered pussy against my thigh, seeking any type of friction to satisfy her arousal. My fingers dip inside each cup of her bra and pull down, freeing her perky tits. My mouth descends on her left nipple, sucking and biting on the hard nub while my hand grips and squeezes the right. I swirl my tongue around the hard peak before releasing it with a pop. Then I repeat the motion on the right.

"Fuck. Your tits are perfection." I continue to kiss and suck my way around each breast as Parisa's moans and pants become louder.

Parisa grips my jaw with her thumb and pointer finger and turns my face to hers and looks me directly in the eyes. "Seth, I'm only going to say this once. If I don't orgasm, I might commit murder."

"We can't have that now, can we?" From the corner of my eye, I see my phone light up with a message. "Damn, Trey," I mutter under my breath.

"What's wrong?"

"Just Trey being… Trey. Enough about him. Time to get back to more important things." I bend at the knees and press my shoulder into Parisa's stomach and lift. She lets out a squeal as she dangles upside down and her hands grip my waist for balance. I wrap one arm around the back of her thighs to make sure she doesn't fall and carry her to her bedroom.

The next morning, I stir awake to find a set of arms and legs tangled with mine. A mess of familiar auburn hair rests against my chest. I turn my head, the blue numbers of Parisa's alarm clock illuminate 8:42 a.m. I'm not one for sleeping in, so usually when the sun rises, I'm not too far behind. But after last night and Parisa's persistence of an orgasm marathon, I must have needed the extra rest. Untangling myself from Parisa and the comforter, I make quick work to find my clothes and get dressed while Parisa groans and rolls over.

When I make my way out to the kitchen, I spot my phone on the table and decide to see what Trey had to say. Picking up my phone and unlocking it, I'm not greeted with messages from Trey, but instead it's notification after notification of missed calls from my dad, my brother, and my sister. Finally, I get to a text message from my brother and click it open.

MARCUS

Mom's in the hospital.

chapter twenty
Dirty Little Secret

Seth

As soon as I see the message, I collect the rest of my things, and I'm out the door. I feel bad for not waking Parisa to tell her I have to go, but my main focus is on my mom. While running down the three flights of stairs I repeatedly dial my brother, then my dad, then my brother again, but no one answers. There are two hospitals in town, so she has to be at one of those. Luckily, they're close together, so I won't take too long if I guess wrong the first time.

Once I reach the bottom, I shove the door open. A blast of cold air hits my face, my heavy breathing casting a misty cloud in front of me. Tearing open my car door, I jam the key into the ignition and turn. My car sparks to life and I wait a minute before throwing it into drive. I use my handsfree to call my brother one more time and he finally answers.

"Marcus, where's Mom?"

"Oh, look who decided to use their phone."

"I was busy. Which hospital are you at?"

"Too busy to answer your phone even after repeated phone calls?"

"Dammit, Marcus! Which hospital?"

"Saint Joseph's."

"I'll be there in five." I end the call, not wanting to deal with him anymore. While mom was in the hospital, I was too busy exchanging orgasms all night to check my phone. If that doesn't make a person feel like shit, I don't know what else would.

I stare as my mom's motionless body as she lies in the hospital bed, resting. The sound of the rhythmic beeping of the machines fills the room. A hand grips my shoulder and I turn to see my dad, exhaustion etched in his features.

"Doctors say it was a heart attack. They're going to run a few more tests, but it doesn't sound like it was too serious."

"What kind of heart attack isn't serious?"

"It could have been worse, much worse."

"She's too young to have a heart attack."

"They suspect it was stress induced. I'm guessing it's because of everything with The Lilith House, between finding a new building, and dealing with repairs to the current one. Your mom will be out of commission for a bit, so we could really use all the help we can get."

"Yeah. Anything."

My parents have always wanted us to be involved with

The Lilith House. For years they would drop subtle hints about us helping. At first it was we should volunteer, and then it was we should take charge one day a week, then they threw legal documents in my direction to help them sort through. But now this. There's no way I can leave them high and dry now. Mom stirs awake and I rush to her side. I tell her I'm here before the nurse comes in to check on her. Dad escorts me to the waiting room where my sister, Brielle, and Marcus are waiting. Annoyed with my older brother, I take the chair next my sister.

"It's about time you get here, yeesh." Brielle looks up from her phone.

"I don't need you on my case, too, Bri."

"Where were you anyway?"

"Does it matter?"

"Wait…" Bri leans in and sniffs me. "You smell like peaches. Were you with a girl?" she says in a hushed whisper. But apparently not quite enough because Marcus overhears.

"You were with a girl last night? You were too busy to come to the hospital because you were with a girl? Unbelievable." He shakes his head at me from across the aisle in disappointment.

"It wasn't like that."

"Then what was it? Because to me it sounds like you were only thinking of yourself."

"You know what? I don't need this shit from you," I spit out before shoving to my feet and stomping to the other side of the room. My stride stops as soon as I'm standing in front of a glass wall that overlooks the lake. Maybe my brother is right. I am selfish. If I hadn't been with Parisa all night I wouldn't have ignored my phone and I would have been here sooner. My jaw clenches so hard I'm surprised I don't crack a molar.

"How are you doing?" Bri elbows me in the ribs as she comes to a halt next to me.

"Meh." I lift one shoulder and let it drop.

"Sorry about Marcus. He's just scared and unfortunately you get to be his punching bag."

"Right now, I can't blame him. I should have been here."

"So, do you have a girlfriend?" Bri beams up at me with a mischievous grin. She was the unplanned pregnancy, so being ten years younger than me she never saw me with a girlfriend.

I huff out a laugh. "I have no idea."

"How can you not know if you have a girlfriend?"

"It's complicated." I cross my arms over my chest and stare up at the ceiling. What are we? We never discussed it. We spent all our time only swapping orgasms. "She's hot one minute, cold the next. She likes me, or I think she does, but also doesn't want anyone to know."

"Wow. Is she embarrassed or something? If a guy did that to me, I'd kick him to the curb. I'm no one's dirty little secret. You shouldn't be either." Bri rests her hand on my forearm. When I look down, I'm met with sympathetic eyes. All I can do is give her a tight-lipped smile then she turns around and returns to her chair.

I stand there for a few more minutes, tuning out the world around me. No hushed voices of family members waiting to see loved ones, no doctors and nurses giving orders, no rubber soled shoes squeaking along the tile floor. Just me and my guilt-ridden thoughts.

My phone buzzes. Digging it out of my pocket I unlock it and see a message from Parisa.

I contemplate how to respond. How much of an explanation do I owe her? It's not like we're dating. This whole thing is just casual. In fact, it's so casual she doesn't want anyone to know.

After I press send, I turn my phone off. I have enough to worry about right now and Parisa is not on the top of that list. When I return to the seating area, I take a seat across from my brother. I rest my elbows on my knees and look up to him.

"I'm sorry I wasn't here last night. I should have been, and I wasn't. I take responsibility for that. But I'm here now for whatever Mom and Dad need."

Marcus mimics my pose. "Good. Mom and Dad are going to be busy for a while and they need help running The Lilith House."

chapter twenty-one
There Goes The
Best Thing

Parisa

"We've been trying to hang out with you for the past week, where have you been?" Olivia sets her half empty margarita glass down on the wood top of our usual table at Porter's. Even on a Sunday, patrons fill all the tables and barstools.

"I've been… busy." I take a quick drink so I don't have to answer any more questions.

"Busy as in work busy or busy getting it on?" Olivia asks before taking a drink of her own.

"If I had to guess by the way her cheeks turned the same color as her hair, it's the latter," Charlie says as she points her drink in my direction.

I can't lie to my best friends, but I could always omit the truth. That's not lying, right? "If you must know. Yes, it's a guy, but it's nothing serious." I shrug, the lie more sour than the lime in my drink. Why do I feel so dirty? If I consider "nothing serious" as I can't stop thinking about him or wanting to touch him or kiss him, then sure, it's nothing serious. If I keep telling myself that, it must be true, right?

"Are you keeping a guy from us? Tell us everything." Olivia leans in as if she wants all the dirty details.

"We want to see where it goes before we start telling people." I twirl my straw around in my glass of vodka limeade, needing something to do so I don't tell them the truth.

"What does he look like? What's his name? What does he do?" Olivia starts rapid firing the questions at me, and I freeze. I'm unable to think of an answer that would get her off my back, so I spit out the first thing that pops into my head.

"His name is Josh. He has dark hair and he's an engineer. He travels a lot for work, so I don't get to see him often, which is why I couldn't hang out all week." The words just tumble out of my mouth and I'm not fully aware of what I even said. I hope they don't ask me again later. But my answer seems to appease Olivia as she's now stopped with her twenty questions and moved the conversation to more neutral topics like ones not involving my love life.

Shortly after our second round of drinks arrive at the table, I look up to see Bennett and Trey sauntering our way and of course, trailing not so far behind them is Seth. Bennett grabs a stool and cozies up next to Charlie while Trey takes a seat next to Olivia. Great, that leaves the only open spot for Seth next to me. I give him a tight-lipped smile as he sits down, not wanting to tip anyone off. Luckily, they all seem to be preoccupied with their own conversations to see the sexual energy radiating from this end of the table.

"So, did you hear Parisa has been keeping a secret guy from us?" Olivia raises an eyebrow while everyone else turns their heads in my direction. Dammit. What is she doing?

"Oh, I think we need to meet this guy to see if he's qualified to hang with our tribe here." Trey does a circle motion around the table with this finger.

"You're the boyfriend police now? Whatever you say, *Dad*," I say to Trey.

"That's daddy to you." Trey winks at me.

I crumple my napkin and throw it in his direction. "You're a pig. But I wouldn't put it past you to make your hook ups call you daddy."

"Only when they've been bad girls."

"On second thought, I would rather not know about the girls you hook up with."

"If you want, we can go out back and I'll let you call me daddy." Trey gives me a head nod.

From the corner of my eye, I see the whites of Seth's knuckles as he grips his glass of beer. I swear, if he squeezes any harder our table is going to be covered in beer and shards of glass.

"I'll pass on that, but thanks, Trey."

"Plus, she's seeing some super-hot engineer named Josh," Olivia spits out.

"Yeah, she's been with him all week. I'm surprised we've been able to snag her for one night. But we want to know more," Charlie says.

Olivia leans in. "Yes girl, spill it."

"I… uh…" I look over to Seth, he stands and slams his glass on the table.

"If you'll excuse me. I'll be right back."

He pushes away from the table and zig zags his way through the crowd toward the bar. When my gaze shifts back to the table all eyes are on me. Fuck. If they didn't have a suspicion before, they do now.

"I'll be right back." I stand and follow Seth's path through the crowd.

What could he be so mad about? He knew we were keeping this a secret. He can't possibly believe I'm seeing someone else. By the time I finally reach him he's already down the dark hallway leading to the back exit. I reach out and grab his elbow to get his attention. He whirls around and I'm met with stormy emerald eyes.

"What happened back there? You have to believe me when I say I'm not seeing anyone else."

Seth looks up to the ceiling before his gaze drifts back to mine. "Look, I know you're not seeing anyone else—"

"Then what's the problem?"

"You know what the problem is? I'm tired of hiding this." He points between the two of us. "I'm tired of only getting half of you. The half when we're alone. I want to tell the world that this smart, funny, and amazingly beautiful woman wants to be with me, and I am the luckiest guy in the world because of that. But instead, I get jealous over a fictitious guy because he's the one you tell your friends about. I'm tired of being your dirty little secret. I think I deserve more than that."

"Seth, you know why I don't want to tell anyone. At least not yet. People will talk and all the rumors will start."

"If you knew anything about me, then you would know I'm not like your ex."

Seth's glare bores into me but I have nothing to say. No words to reassure him that everything he's saying is true. He's not like my ex. Except I say nothing.

"I thought so," he spits out. He turns on his heel but

before he's out the door he turns around. "I was hoping we could talk tonight because I really needed you. But instead, I learned where I stand. Chasing a girl who is clearly embarrassed to be with me."

My shoulders drop. "Seth, that's not true."

"But isn't it?" He raises an eyebrow waiting for my response.

"I'm sorry."

"Yeah. Me too." He turns and his hand slams into the door as he storms through. I watch as the door closes, shrouding me in darkness again. Tears flood my eyes. I just fucked up the best thing that's happened to me.

chapter twenty-two

I'm Not Going Anywhere

Parisa

The following day, I head into work a few minutes early to hopefully catch Seth. I spent all night tossing and turning, hating the way things went down last night. With each step, my heels pound against the concrete sidewalk. Flakes of snow swirl around as I duck my head and wrap my arms around myself to fight the bitter, icy wind. No matter how long I've lived in Northern Minnesota I will never get used to the winters.

The murmur of voices and soft chanting draws my attention, causing me to look up. Standing in front of The Blue Stone Group is a crowd of fifteen to twenty people, several of them holding signs while others hand out pieces of paper to anyone who passes by. I shuffle my way through the crowd until I reach the glass doors, when someone shoves a flyer into my face. Grabbing it, I hold it out and read the big bold words on the front.

Once I reach the front door, Gary, the middle-aged security guard is holding the door open for me. "Are you alright Ms. Anthony? The crowd hasn't gotten too unruly, have they?"

"No, I'm fine. Thank you. When did they show up?" I point behind me.

"A few have been here since about five a.m. and it's been steadily growing ever since. It will be best if you use the parking garage entrance until this settles down."

"Thanks, Gary. I'll do that."

So, this must be the controversy that The Blue Stone Group has caused in the community. There've been whispers around the office that they purchased a large lot and plan to level it and build some condos or something. But according to this flyer, a city park is also the casualty of another housing complex. As I walk toward the bank of elevators, I tuck the paper into my bag. I can only deal with one crisis at a time and right now, my main one is Seth.

My head is a mess, and I don't know what to do. He's not answering any of my calls or text messages, but if I run into him in person he has to talk to me. I check the clock and it's 7:30 a.m. By the time 7:45 rolls around there is still no sign of Seth. Everything on his desk is in the same spot as he left it on Friday. 7:55 a.m and he's still nowhere to be found. It's not like him to be late. What if something happened? I stare at the clock for the next five minutes and when it changes to 8:00, Seth's desk chair is still empty.

"Parisa, may I have a word with you in my office? It's about your application for the Marketing Director position." Mr. Evans startles me.

"Yes. I'll be right there." I take one last glance at Seth's desk before I push my chair in and walk to Mr. Evans' office. When I arrive, the door is open a crack, but I still knock softly before peeking my head in. "You wanted to see me?"

"Parisa. Please come in and shut the door behind you." Mr. Evans doesn't even look up from his computer.

Slowly, I round the door and close it behind me before taking a seat in front of the large mahogany executive desk. I intertwine my fingers in my lap as I wait for him to finish his typing. My heart thunders in my chest as a bead of sweat forms on my brow. This can only go one of two ways. He called me in here to tell me I got the promotion, or I'm fired and it's Seth's and he's not here today because he's out celebrating. Both of those scenarios cause a knot the size of a bowling ball to form in the pit of my stomach.

"Thanks for coming in. Sorry it has taken us so long to come to a decision. A lot of things have come up that caused us to postpone the decision. But you've done some outstanding work for us, and we would like to offer you the marketing director position."

A wide smile covers my face. I got the promotion. I can't believe I got it. I'm internally doing a happy dance.

"Thank you so much, Mr. Evans. I promise I won't let you or the company down."

"I know you won't. We'll get all the paperwork ready for you and get you settled into your new office later this week." Mr. Evans stands and rounds his desk and I follow suit. Mindlessly, I trail behind him as we make our way toward the door.

"Oh wow. My own office." I envision how I'll decorate… My. Own. Office. Will I have a view of the lake? Maybe I'll get the morning sun or perhaps the afternoon light? Mr. Evans stops in front of the open doorway, startling me. "Thank you again. One question. Does that mean Seth got the assistant position?"

"You didn't hear? Seth put in his resignation this morning. We'll have to find someone else for the assistant position."

"Oh." I try to keep the disappointment out of my voice, but fail. Seth quit. He didn't even say anything. Did he know I was getting the position and didn't want to work under me? His ego couldn't handle that I won and he lost. By the time I'm walking back to my cubicle I'm no longer sad Seth left, instead I'm fuming.

Once I reach my desk, I sit down and shake my mouse to wake up my computer. My leg bounces as I wait for the screen to load. That jerk couldn't even tell me himself. He took the coward's way out. My fingers shake as I pick up my phone. Then I slam it back down. No, he can't get away with this. I pick up the phone again and start to dial his number, but slam the phone back down.

I jump from my seat and stride toward the elevator. Olivia is downstairs and I need someone to talk me off this ledge. I jam my finger into the down button and the elevator opens. The thirty second ride to the first floor does nothing to cool my temper. My heels echo as each step stomps on the marble floor.

"That son of a bitch quit!"

A wide-eyed Olivia turns around with a phone pressed to her ear. "Yes, Ms. Day. I have you down for Wednesday." She pauses while I mouth *sorry*. "Okay. See you then." Olivia sets the phone on the receiver. "What are you talking about?"

"Seth quit. That son of a bitch quit. He couldn't handle that I got the promotion and he didn't, so he quit."

"Well one, you got the promotion!" Olivia squeals with delight and claps her hands. "But two, Seth quit?"

"Thank you. And yes! Mr. Evans called me into his office to offer me the position and when I asked if Seth got the assistant job, he told me he quit."

"That doesn't seem like Seth to just quit. Did he know he wasn't going to get it?"

"I don't know. We got into a fight. He won't answer any of my calls so all I can guess is that he can't handle the idea that I beat him."

Olivia stands up, palms on the desk, and leans forward with an eyebrow raised. "Back up the gossip train. You and Seth always fight but why are you repeatedly calling him?"

I blow out an exasperated breath. "Well, we didn't tell anyone but we've maybe, kind of, been seeing each other."

"Shut up!" Olivia slams her palms on the desk.

"I know. I never expected it to happen either but—"

"No. Not that. Trey was right."

"What?" I furrow my brows.

"We all had an idea something was happening between you two. And it was Trey who mentioned it."

"Oh. So, when I thought we were hiding it, everyone actually knew?"

"Pretty much." Olivia lifts one shoulder and lets it fall and leans forward. "But give me the deets."

"Deets on what?" A familiar, masculine voice sounds from behind me before propping himself on the desk next to me.

"How everyone knew about Seth and Parisa," Olivia states.

"Oh, how she's been banging the polka dots off his bow tie."

I smack Trey in the stomach, which is followed by an oomph. "Can you be a little more discreet?"

"Why? Everyone already knows." We all turn to the new girl and she nods her head confirming she also knows.

I roll my eyes. "Is nothing a secret around here?" I pause knowing they will hound me until I tell them everything. "Where do I start?"

"Does he also wear a bow tie around his dick?" Trey raises an eyebrow.

"Really? That's your question? He's your friend, can't you ask him yourself?" I ask.

"There are some topics of conversation guys avoid. One of those is dick accessories. But you can tell me." Trey makes a zipper motion across his lips. I'm tempted to smack him again, but it might be crossing the line into assault.

"The first time was in Colorado and then a few more times afterward…"

"Just a few?" Trey raises an eyebrow.

I release an exasperated sigh. "Ugh! Fine. Like ten. But I completely messed everything up."

"By creating a fake boyfriend." Olivia scrunches up her nose.

"Yeah, that. But now he's not answering any of my messages. I've even gone to his house, but he's never home.

After waiting two hours, I'm pretty sure his neighbors think I'm a stalker and have given the police my license plate."

Trey rests his elbow on the counter. "After the news about his mom, I know he's been spending a lot of time over there and at The Lilith House. I'm pretty sure he's working there tonight."

"Why didn't I think of that? You're the best, Trey." I wrap my arms around his neck and squeeze. After I release him, he turns to Olivia.

"Did you hear that? I'm the best."

She just shakes her head. They continue their banter as I bolt toward the elevator to get back to my desk. Maybe I can fake an illness to get out of work early?

I didn't fake an illness, but I did fake a gynecologist appointment that I just so happened to forget about. Hopefully, I won't have any real reason to visit for at least another six months. I throw my car in park and jump out. Pulling open the door I walk down a familiar hallway. The clanking of pots and pans grows louder with each step while the smell of cornbread fills my nostrils. When I round the corner, I see him. His hair is slightly disheveled and tiredness surrounds his eyes. He stands behind the buffet style table and directs volunteers on what they should be doing.

My heart feels like it's going to beat out of my chest. With careful movements, like a teenager trying to sneak into the house, I enter the large dining room, hopeful that I'm quiet enough so he doesn't hear me. A spoon falls off the table and hits the floor with a clatter. He bends down to retrieve it, and while he's still on the ground, I clear my throat.

"Sorry, but we're not open yet. It will be another thirty minutes," Seth says from underneath the table.

"Actually, I'm here to talk to you."

Seth bolts upright, his back going ramrod straight at the sound of my voice. A look of shock and surprise covers his features before he narrows his eyes at me. "I don't have time to talk. I'm a little busy here." He turns and walks the line down the tables, and I follow on the opposite side.

"Please Seth. Hear me out."

"What could you possibly have to say? I miss you, but hey, I don't want to tell anyone about you because I'm embarrassed to be with you."

The bite to his tone causes me to flinch. "It wasn't like that."

"Then what was it?" He stops dead in his tracks and crosses his arms over his chest.

Not knowing what to say or how to say it because as bad as it sounds, it's just like that. Maybe not embarrassed but I didn't need the rumor starting. Without thinking, the next few words tumble out of my mouth. "I got the promotion."

Seth huffs, then sneers, "Well, congratulations. You got everything you wanted." Like a child throwing a tantrum, he stomps away, slamming his fist into the two-way swinging door leading into the kitchen.

A lone tear pricks my eye and cascades down my cheek. I swipe it away and walk back the way I came in. When I'm almost to the exit a familiar voice calls out.

"Hey Parisa. Wait." Turning around, Maggie is standing at the end of the hall. With an apron still draped around her neck she walks up to me. "It's so great to see you again."

"Well, I'm glad someone thinks so." I give her a lopsided smile.

"Seth's had a rough week. He'll come around."

"I'm not so sure about that."

"I've known Seth since he was knee high. Watched him grow up into the outstanding man he is today and let me tell you, I've never seen him as smitten with anyone else as I've seen him with you. You are the light to his darkness and right now there's a lot of darkness. Don't give up on him. He needs you more than ever right now."

I sigh. As much as I want to believe he needs me, it's hard to believe it when he ignores me. "I don't know what to do. He won't even talk to me."

"Just be there for him. Let him know you're there for whenever he's ready to get his head out of his ass." Maggie gives me a wink.

I chuckle, but I let her words sink in. On the surface Seth may never want to see me again but I know deep down his feelings for me run just as deep as mine do for him. Maggie's right. I need to let him know that I'm here for him and I'm not going anywhere, whether he likes it or not.

"Do you have an extra apron?"

chapter twenty-three
One Day At A Time

Seth

Why did she have to come here? Just when I've stopped spending every moment thinking about her, she shows up to invade my thoughts once again. Then to rub salt in my wounds, she tells me she got the promotion. To be fair, I did quit and even if they did offer it to me, I would have turned it down anyway. Either way, I don't care about the job, the promotion, or her. I repeatedly jam the masher into the pot of potatoes.

"What did those potatoes do to you?"

Frustrated, I toss the masher into the sink. "Nothing." I lean back against the counter as Maggie gives me sympathetic eyes. "I don't know what to do anymore. About anything."

"Don't be so hard on yourself." She rests her hand on

my forearm. "A lot has happened in the last week. Your mom is very lucky to have you. You just need to take it one day at a time."

I nod and give her a tight smile. Maggie has always been like a second mom to me and often a voice of reason, especially when it's unsolicited. But she's right. Take it one day at a time.

"I'm going to bring these out to the line." I finish scooping the potatoes into a buffet pan and carry them out to the service area. Just as the door swings closed behind me, I look up and I'm greeted with familiar auburn locks sitting in a pile on top of her head wrapped in a hair net as a white apron drapes around her neck. She's not the distraction I need.

I take a few steps and drop the pan into the tray. The loud noise causes her to turn around. When she notices the scowl on my face, the smile on hers falls.

"I thought you were leaving."

Uncertainty flits across her face before she composes herself. "I'm here to volunteer."

"This isn't your thing."

"But this is exactly where I want to be."

"We have enough volunteers," I lie. Because I don't know if I'll be able to control myself with her so close.

"I'm sure you could use one more." She shifts back and forth on her feet.

"Nope. We're all good."

"But who's serving the sides?"

"Lance will."

At the sound of his name Lance looks up. "But I'm serving desserts."

Sara, another volunteer, walks by. "Then Sara will."

Just then Maggie steps out of the kitchen. Her gaze locks onto Parisa before drifting to me. "Sara, I need your help in the kitchen. Parisa can take the sides." A knowing smile passes across Parisa's lips as Maggie gives her a wink.

What the hell just happened? These two are conspiring against me. Now I have to spend the next couple of hours standing next to the girl who looks absolutely stunning, even in a hairnet. The girl who constantly invites herself into my dreams. And whose peach scent makes my dick hard. Son of a bitch. This apron will do more than just keep my clothes clean.

The first thirty minutes carry on without a hitch. I keep my eyes to myself even though I'm tempted to look in her direction every time her sugary sweet voice greets every person who comes through the line. And her laugh. God, I miss her laugh. And the way her nose crinkles with each giggle.

"Well, if it isn't my favorite person." When I look up, Lenard shuffles his feet until he's standing in front of Parisa giving her a wide grin.

"I see how it is. Just forgot about all those games of Euchre we've played together," I say.

"If you looked as pretty as this one, you could be my favorite person." He goes back to schmoozing Parisa.

"Would you at least like some ham?" Without even turning to me, he holds out his tray in my direction. With a shake of my head, I exhale a laugh and toss of piece of ham on top of his cafeteria style tray.

"I'm glad to see you back here. This one," Lenard nods in my direction, "has been a grump while you've been away. Permanent scowl on his face."

Apparently, today is "throw Seth under the bus" day.

"I'll have you know it's not a permanent scowl. Life has been a little busy lately."

"It's not his fault. It's actually mine," Parisa confesses. "I said something I didn't mean. So, his hurt feelings are completely valid. I just want him to know I'm sorry and I'll do whatever it takes to make amends. Even if that means we can only be friends." Parisa turns toward me, a pleading look on her face.

I know I should forgive her. She's left countless messages apologizing, but it's hard when it's a person who's stolen your heart and won't give it back. But also, it's not like I want it back either.

"What are you waiting for? Forgive the girl already. Because let me tell you something. If you don't snatch this one up, someone else will. Then you *will* have a permanent scowl on your face, and it won't be because I beat you in Euchre." He shakes his finger at me like he's scolding a toddler.

I press my lips together. I know he's right. Parisa can have her choice of any man in the world and right now, she here with me, serving food in an apron and a hairnet. "Thanks for the advice, Mr. Rickett."

Lenard continues down the line, snagging two cookies before he sits down at his usual table. We finish serving the rest of the line while an awkwardness lingers in the air. Maybe I need to accept her apology, then we can all move on.

Once everyone's trays are full, we begin our clean up. I reach for a tray at the same moment Parisa does. Her fingers rest on top of mine. The touch sends an electric current through my entire body. My gaze remains fixated on her hand before drifting up to her face. When her eyes meet mine, the same magnetic pull I feel swirls in her irises. What seems to last for minutes is only seconds before I pull my hand away. She mutters a quick sorry and makes her way to the next tray. I watch as she lifts the tray and strolls past me before disappearing behind the kitchen door. Resting my hands on the table I bow my head, inhaling a deep breath. My head and my heart are at war with each other. I spend every waking second thinking about her but then a bucket of cold water is thrown on me every time I think back to the night at the bar. My sister is right, I shouldn't be anyone's dirty little secret.

"Hey Seth." Maggie's voice interrupts my self loathing. "We have most of the kitchen cleaned up minus a few of the dishes. Parisa volunteered to stay back to help finish. Also, before you leave, your dad mentioned cutting the power to the dishwasher. It's been acting up again and he just wants to make sure nothing happens before he can get someone out to look at it."

I nod. "Thanks Maggie." She turns and disappears down the hallway. The door latching closed echoes down the empty corridor. Shit. The last thing I wanted was to be stuck here all by myself with Parisa. It's easy to be distracted with other people around but when it's just the two of us… I can only fight it so long before I want to feast on the temptation. I pick up the last tray and carry it into the kitchen. Parisa is loading everything into the dishwasher. She turns around when she hears the swinging door close.

"Maggie said she needed to get home so I told her I would stay. Hope that's okay?"

"Yeah. Thanks for offering."

Parisa turns back around and presses the start button. I hold my breath as the machine starts up and the dishes slowly feed through, everything seeming normal. In the meantime, Parisa heads to the closet for the rest of the cleaning supplies and we get to work. An uncomfortable silence fills the room as I wipe down the counter tops and she mops the floor.

While staring at my rag I break the silence. "Congratulations on the promotion. You deserve it. I know you would have gotten it whether I stayed or left."

"Thanks. But… why did you up and quit?"

I pinch my eyes shut before looking up to her. She's standing on the other side of the stainless steel worktable, mop still in hand, head tilted to the side, curiosity written all over her face. "My family needed me. The night at the bar, when you told everyone you were seeing some fake guy, I was there to tell you that my mom was in the hospital."

"Oh Seth. I'm so sorry. I wish you would have told me."

"My head was a jumbled mess with my mom and then after what you said… I figured it was just easier to leave."

"I get that. What happened with your mom?"

"She had a mild heart attack. She's on the mend. But I needed to step up and help with The Lilith House. That's why I quit. My family needed me to step in. But this works out for everyone now." I continue wiping down the surface, mostly to distract myself from spilling my true feelings.

"I guess so," Parisa says, her voice somber as she continues mopping.

Every time she walks past me, I get a whiff of her peach scent and it makes me want to lift her up on the table and kiss the hell out of her just like last time we were here. Instead, I stand here wiping the same spot over and over again. I have so many things I want to say but I don't know how to say them.

"If you keep that up, I'm afraid you're going to scrub a hole right through the metal."

When I look her way, Parisa hoists herself onto the

table next to me. Her legs dangle off the side. She reaches up and tugs her hair loose from her ponytail. Auburn strands cascade down her shoulders. It's times like these when I want to run my fingers through those luscious locks and tug, forcing her to look at me. I want to take what's mine. I shake the thought from my head because she's not mine. She won't let me be hers. I walk past her to throw my rag into the sink, but she stops me with her hand on my arm.

"Seth." Her gaze drops to the floor before meeting mine. "I hate things are weird between us. I wish things could just go back to the way they were."

"Me too. But it's hard to forget what you said."

"I know. And I'm sorry. The ex has found a way to ruin my life even after we broke up." She lets out a humorless laugh and drops her head.

I place a finger under her chin and force her to look at me. "That guy's an asshole for many reasons. You deserve so much better than him."

"Clearly not, since I've messed this up, too."

I bend down so I'm eye level with her. "Parisa, you are a bright, intelligent, amazing, beautiful woman. Don't let yourself think otherwise."

Her eyes search mine. With each passing second her lips get closer and closer to mine. It's hard to tell if I'm the one moving closer or her. But in the last second our lips crash into each other, mouths fused together. I wrap my hand around the back of her neck to draw her closer to me and she comes willingly. My tongue strokes and caresses hers. She wraps her arms around my neck like she's afraid I might let go. If I had it my way, I would *never* let her go.

Suddenly, there's a loud clacking noise behind me followed by the sound of gushing water splashing on the floor. Pulling away, I rush over to the dishwasher and quickly press the stop button. Everything comes to a grinding halt. Within a few seconds Parisa's at my side with a handful of towels.

"Dammit. Of course, this would have to happen." I huff.

"Hey. We got this. Nothing we haven't done before." Parisa throws a small smile in my direction, and it makes me feel slightly better about the situation. Hurriedly, I turn off the water supply while Parisa cleans up the water. I remove all the unwashed dishes and place them in the sink.

An hour later everything is back to normal. All the water is mopped up and the remaining dishes have been washed and put away. I lean against the counter and Parisa follows suit. When I turn toward her, she lets out a big yawn.

I look down at my watch and notice the time. "Shit. I'm sorry. I've kept you later than expected."

"No worries. I wasn't going to make you clean this up by yourself."

"Thanks for staying and helping today."

"Would it make me a horrible person if I said I did it to see you?"

Silence fills the room as I try to think of something to say.

"Sorry, that was probably crossing the line." She pushes off the counter and heads into the office to collect her belongings.

"Just give me a minute to shut the lights off and I'll walk you out."

"Okay."

Running to the office, I snag my keys and turn all the lights off. I meet up with Parisa in the hallway and we walk down together. Opening the door, she walks past me, and I secure the door by locking the deadbolt. When I turn around Parisa wraps her arms around herself in an attempt to stay warm in the cold.

"You didn't need to wait."

"I wanted to." Her warm breath sends a misty fog into the air.

I nod my head and escort her through the moonlit parking lot. Once she's close enough to her car, she presses the button on her key fob unlocking her doors. She pulls the handle and I finish opening it the rest of the way. Before getting in, she turns around and looks up at me. My eyes shift back and forth between hers before moving down. My gaze lingering on her lips. Her tongue peeks out before she nibbles on her bottom lip. I can't help but stare in fascination, wanting to be the one to nibble on that lip. A dog barking in the distance pulls me from my trance.

"Thanks for staying tonight," I say, my voice is low.

"You said that already."

A small smile tugs at my lips. "I did, didn't I?"

She gives me a weak smile of her own. "Well, I better get going."

"Yeah. Me too."

Parisa stretches up on her tippy toes and tilts her head to the side. Instinctively, I turn my head at the same time and our lips meet. Soft and supple. And for the briefest moment I want to say forget everything that's happened and tell her to come home with me. God knows my dick is screaming at me to do that very thing. Just as quickly as the kiss started, it's over. Parisa pulls away, uncertainty etched across her face.

"Sorry. I shouldn't have done that." Her fingers press against her lips like she's wanting to hold on to the feeling for a moment longer.

"No. It's my fault. I turned my head when clearly you were going for my cheek."

"Yeah. Well, goodnight."

"Goodnight."

This time, I let her get into her car. Once she's seated, I shut the door. The sound of the engine roars to life and I take a step back as she reverses out of the parking spot. I watch as she exits the parking lot, her red taillights disappearing into the dark night.

When I reach my car, I open the door, and climb inside. I start the engine and while it idles, I think back to the whole evening. Parisa's unexpected arrival just so she could talk to me. The two kisses we shared. There's an undeniable pull between us and I'm starting to lose my grasp on why I continue to deny it.

"Shit," I mumble to myself, remembering some loan documents I left on the desk in the office. I turn off my car and make my way back inside.

chapter twenty-four
One Night And It's Gone

Parisa

I stir awake to the beeping of my alarm clock. Turning over, I repeatedly smack the top button until the persistent noise stops. I roll back over when visions of yesterday flit through my mind. Seeing Seth. The kiss in the kitchen. The kiss at my car. My lips pull into a full smile from the memory. He has this magical ability to turn me into a giddy teenager and it excites me and terrifies me all at the same time. I've never felt so drawn to a person before, not only physically, but mentally as well. He makes me want to be a better person every day.

Running off the high from yesterday, I saunter into my closet and pick out a fun and flirty outfit, an oversized blush sweater, dark skinny jeans, and tan booties and set it on my bed. Exiting my bedroom, I take the short walk down the hallway to hop in the shower. The warm water cascades over my body and I can't wash away the permanent smile on my face. Once I'm finished, I wrap my fluffy bathrobe around me and finish my morning routine of blow drying my hair, applying my light make up, and getting dressed. I peel back the blackout curtains, the morning sun warming my face. As I walk into my kitchen, the automatic coffee maker beeps, the warm vanilla aroma informing me it's ready. After I collect everything I need for work, I head out of my apartment.

As I saunter into The Blue Stone Group, I'm still fighting to keep the smile off my face. All I have to do is think of Seth and butterflies take flight in my belly. Instantly, that feeling evaporates when I see the look on Olivia's face as she talks to Trey. Her brows are furrowed, concern etched on her features. I hurry my pace until I'm standing next to Trey, eyes fixed on Olivia.

"What's wrong?" Then I turn to Trey. "Will someone tell me what's wrong?"

"Uh… well…" Trey wraps his hand around the back of his neck.

My gaze darts back to Olivia. "Did you see the news this morning?"

"No, I didn't see the news. What happened?" Panic laces my voice. Whenever someone asks if you've seen the news, it's never good.

Olivia looks to Trey before turning to me. "There was a fire last night, at The Lilith House—"

All my thoughts fly to Seth. He was there with me last night, but I left before him. "Where's Seth? Is he alright?"

Panic seizes up my throat and my palms get clammy. I left before Seth. What if he went back inside? White spots pop up as my vision fades. I rest my hand on the desk for balance as my entire body sways to the left. Suddenly, hands are gripping me, and I'm being lowered onto a chair. Muffled voices surround me as if I'm in the classroom with Charlie Brown's teacher. Someone shoves a bottle of water at my face and tells me to drink it. The cool water hits my lips, pulling me back into the present.

Finally, Trey puts me out of my misery. "Seth's fine. Everyone's fine. The place was empty, but the building is a total loss."

Olivia pulls out her phone, her fingers swipe across the screen, then she's handing it to me. Immediately my eyes scan the headline *Late Night Fire Destroys Local Community Shelter* before traveling down to the picture. The entire backside of the building has collapsed in. Half of the north and west walls are standing. Smoke lingers in the air as ashes still smolder. In one night, everything is gone. For a brief moment I feel relieved Seth is okay. That everyone is okay but then it hits me. They lost everything. My words are non-existent. I feel completely and utterly helpless.

"Do they know what happened?" I pass Olivia her phone back.

"We haven't heard anything yet," Trey replies

"I should call Seth. I'm going to call Seth." Before they can respond, I stand on wobbly legs and turn, the clacking of my booties echoing through the open atrium drowning out the thoughts in my head. Once in the elevator I pull out my phone and find Seth's number. My finger hovers over the call button, unsure of what I should say. *Sorry about your family's foundation burning to the ground but I can't stop thinking about our kiss.* Shit. I'm an asshole. I toss my phone back into my bag and lean my head against the wall. The ding from the elevator when it stops on my floor pulls me from my self-deprecation. My legs propel me down the hall like I'm on autopilot and my destination is programmed into my brain. I tune out all the chatter and people milling around me.

Once I reach my new office, I walk through the threshold and softly close it behind me. I slump against the wood and slide down to the floor, needing a few minutes of silence to collect my thoughts. With my bag next to me, contents spilled on the floor, I find my phone and pull up Seth's number again. This time I press the talk button. My heart feels like it's going to pound right out of my rib cage. It rings and rings until finally his voicemail picks up.

"Hi Seth, I just heard the news. I'm so sorry. If there's anything I can help with, let me know. Call me back."

I press the end button but still feel unsatisfied. Rising to my feet I walk to my desk, take a seat, and try to distract myself with work.

Several hours pass and I feel like I've accomplished nothing. I stare at my phone sitting on my desk and it's been crickets all morning, minus Charlie sending me a message about the fire. But Seth still hasn't returned my call so this time I send him a quick message.

PARISA

Sorry to hear about the fire. Glad no one was hurt. Please give me a call.

Again, I wait, but this time I can see he's opened my message but still no response.

All afternoon I continue to check my phone, but my message remains unanswered. I'm at a loss on what to do. Looking back, I know I've made several mistakes that I wish I could take back. He's been the only guy who's ever been there for me, truly been there, and all I did was keep him at arm's length. I can't blame him for not wanting to talk to me. Somehow, I need to show him he means so much more to me than I've given him credit for.

chapter twenty-five
Bring Good Snacks

Seth

When I got the text message from Trey that it was guys night at Porter's, I knew I needed to get out of the house, at least for a few hours. Dealing with the insurance company about the fire has been a headache. Then there's Parisa. She's left me voicemails and messages all day, but I didn't have it in me to message back.

As soon as my shoes hit the pavement, a gust of bitter cold wind rolling off the lake slaps me in the face. I shut my car door, lock it with the key fob, and make my way toward the front door of Porter's. I shove my hands into my coat pockets to fight off the cold. The door opens, a couple strolls out, and I slip inside after them. Immediately, I spot Trey and Bennett sitting at a high-top table left of the bar. I shrug off my coat and make my way toward the familiar faces.

"Hey man. Sorry about the fire." Bennett slides a cold pint of beer in my direction.

"Thanks."

"Has the fire inspector found the cause yet?"

"Nothing yet. Just that it was an electrical fire that started somewhere on the backside. It might be a few more days before we find out anything definite." I lift the glass to my mouth and take a drink, contemplating on saying what I've been thinking all day. "Truth be told, I think the fire was my fault."

Trey and Bennett turn to me simultaneously.

"What are you talking about?" Trey asks.

"Yeah. What are you talking about?" Bennett parrots.

"Fuck." My gaze wanders up to the ceiling before falling back down to my two best friends and I exhale a deep breath. "So, I was getting ready to serve dinner last night and Parisa showed up wanting to talk. I wasn't in the mood to talk, but somehow she weaseled her way into volunteering. Not only that, but volunteering next to me on the serving line. All night she distracted me. Maggie had mentioned something about the dishwasher not working right. It was doing some weird stuff. Someone was coming in later in the week to look at it, so I was going to turn off the breaker before I left, but Parisa distracted me and I forgot." I take another swig of my beer. "It's been eating at me that it's my fault because I didn't take care of that piece of shit dishwasher."

"Hey, Seth. Take it easy. It was an accident." Bennett clasps me on the shoulder.

"It's like the world is punishing me."

"For what?" Trey asks.

"Fuck. I don't know. Wanting to be with the girl instead of staying focused."

"What are you talking about?" Bennett tilts his head.

"First, the night my mom went to the hospital, I was with Parisa. I ignored my phone all night because I thought it was Trey and all his sex jokes. And now this. I was distracted because of Parisa and the foundation burned to the ground."

"Are you blaming Parisa?" Bennett asks.

"No." I scrub my hands down my face. "I don't know. Bad things seem to happen whenever we get close."

"That's some voodoo conspiracy shit," Trey says.

"Look, all that shit is just a coincidence. It means nothing." Bennett takes a drink of his beer.

Trey turns to me. "Are you guys going to rebuild?"

I tap my finger against the glass. "I don't know. Even if we get insurance money, it's nowhere near what it would cost to build something new and furnish it. That was everything my parents worked so hard on. That was their legacy. And in a single night it's gone."

"Sorry, man. If there is anything we can do," Bennett points between him and Trey, "let us know."

"Thanks. I'm tired of talking about this. What's new with you guys?"

Trey and Bennett exchange glances before a Cheshire grin covers Trey's face. "Well, this asshole here is thinking about getting married."

"What? You're asking Charlie to marry you?" I ask wide eyed.

"I think I am. I can't imagine my life without her in it." A starry-eyed look covers Bennett's face.

Trey starts singing "Single Ladies" by Beyoncé while holding his left hand out and shimmying his shoulders.

Bennett slaps his hand away. "Exactly. I'm putting a

ring on it so everyone will know she's mine. I have a meeting with a jeweler next week."

"When are you going to propose?" I ask.

"I'm thinking in the summer. She's always talking about wanting to go sailing and I know a guy with a boat. So, I'll take her out on the lake and ask her to be mine."

"Aww, isn't that some sappy shit?" Trey holds up a finger. "But the only good thing that will come out of a wedding is bridesmaids. You gotta make sure there are some hot, single bridesmaids. Ones who are all feeling insecure about not finding the one, yet all their friends have. I'll swoop in and show them they don't need the one but the one *right now*. But only for a few hours. After that, they expect breakfast and shit."

"So, you want to exploit their feelings for your own pleasure?" I raise an eyebrow at Trey.

"There will be plenty of pleasure for everyone. Don't worry about that. And I like to think they are using me to forget about their problems. So, I'm actually doing *them* a favor."

"I'm going to take immense pleasure when you find a woman you can't live without." I point my beer in Trey's direction.

"Why does everyone keep saying that? SBL forever."

"SBL?" Bennett asks.

"Single Bros Life." Trey reaches for his wallet and pulls out a business card. He looks at Bennett. "You don't get one because you're practically married."

"Damn. I'm so sad," Bennett deadpans.

Then he slides the card to me. "But you're technically single."

My gaze wanders over the embossed lettering.

Single Bros Life

NOTHING IS TYING US DOWN

"We meet Thursday nights. And if you come, bring snacks. The good kind too. Fucking Darren thinks cheese whiz and crackers an are acceptable snack. We are sophisticated men. Bring some brie and fig crostini or some shit."

I bark out at laugh. I don't know if it's because Trey considers himself sophisticated or that he just said brie and fig crostini, maybe both. "Thanks. I'll think about it."

"I'm serious. Good snacks."

I flip the card between my fingers. Only Trey would create a singles guy club. But maybe he's on to something because this club seems easier than dealing with this dumpster fire of emotions right now.

chapter twenty-six
Drinks And
Charity Auctions

Parisa

It's been over twenty-four hours and still no word from Seth.

"Can we find a DeLorean and go back in time and change everything that's happened in the past week?"

One night, *Back to the Future* was streaming so I decided to watch it since Seth said it was his favorite movie and I have to agree, the first two are much better than the third.

I shrug my jacket off and drape it over the back of the bar stool before throwing myself down on the seat next to my sister, Hollyn. I sent an SOS message to her, Charlie, and Olivia that I needed girl time. Hollyn mentioned a new martini bar when I said I wasn't in the mood for Porter's. Vodka drunk it is.

"Here. You need this more than I do." Charlie slides

her lemon drop martini toward me from across the table, then flags down our waitress for another.

I lift the glass to my mouth. The sugary rim hits my lips before I take a heaping gulp, the vodka burning as it flows down my throat. "Thanks. Sadly, I don't think just one's going to cut it."

"It's a good thing we have all night." Olivia raises her drink and Hollyn and I clink our glasses with hers while Charlie raises her water.

"I don't know what to do. Seth won't answer any of my calls or messages. I just want him to know I'm here for him. Whatever he needs." I slowly trace the stem of my martini glass.

Charlie looks to me. "He's got a lot on his plate right now. Bennett mentioned he's been talking to the insurance company and while they don't know what started the fire yet, Seth doesn't think they would get even close to what it would cost to start over."

"That's terrible. They help so many. It would be a huge loss to the community if they didn't open back up," Hollyn says.

"I wish he would just call me. Let me know what I can do to help. Even if it's just to be there for him. He's so stubborn and I hate it." I stare at my almost empty drink.

"I'm sure he will." Charlie reaches across the table and covers my hand with hers for a moment. When she pulls away, she joins Olivia and Hollyn in their conversation.

I'm oblivious to what they're talking about. My thoughts are racing about Seth and what I can do to help him. Then it's like a light bulb goes off. "You guys. I got it. I know what we can do." My outburst causes them to turn their heads in my direction.

"Can you expand on that?" Olivia asks with a raised eyebrow.

"For Seth and The Lilith House. What if we held a charity auction to raise money to help them rebuild?"

"You do realize how much time and energy goes into hosting a charity event, right?" Charlie asks.

"I'm sure it will be a lot but it's worth it. To help *our* friend."

"When you put it that way, I'm in," Charlie says. The other girls follow suit.

"Plus, I'm sure you can do some oral stimulation to convince Bennett to help too. He has a few aces up his sleeve who could make some generous donations." Olivia playfully elbows Charlie.

"What about Trey? What kind of stimulation will be happening there?" Charlie raises an eyebrow.

"Absolutely none. I can't deal with his ever-changing behavior. He's worse than a hormonal teenage girl. Just thinking about it gives me a headache."

"Wait, who's Trey?" Hollyn asks.

"Trey's friends with Bennett and Seth. Loyal to a fault but also doesn't seem to do relationships." Charlie takes a sip of her drink.

"Have you two hooked up?" Hollyn looks to Olivia.

"No. We haven't even kissed. The timing just never seemed right. Sometimes I think we're just better off as friends." Olivia shrugs.

"There's a lot of sexual tension there. I can't believe you haven't banged it out by now," I add.

"I'll admit I'm attracted to him but is that all it is? A physical attraction? I need more than that. But enough about my lacking sex life and back to this event."

"So, you two will talk to the guys about finding donation items for a silent auction." I point to Charlie and Olivia. "Hollyn, maybe The Sweet Spot can donate some desserts?"

Hollyn sits up in her chair. "Yeah, I'll talk to my boss, but I'm sure she would love to help."

"Okay, we'll just need someone who can do catering, maybe just hors d'oeuvres?" I tap my chin.

"And where are we hosting this event?" Charlie asks.

"I bet Jake would let us use Porter's for a night. Plus, the extra exposure for the bar won't be a bad thing," Olivia says.

I pull out my phone and open the notes app. My fingers fly over the keyboard as I type out all the potential businesses we could ask for help. This whole idea is crazy, and it will be even crazier if we can pull it off. I wave down the waitress and order us another round. Once they're set down in front of us, I raise my glass and toast.

"Here's to bringing back The Lilith House and making it bigger and better than before." The other girls raise their glasses. "Also, I think I know how we might be able to secure a new building."

The next day after work, I stride into Porter's. It seems quieter than normal. I must have arrived before the evening crowd. This will give me time to talk to Jake with no distractions. I stroll up to the empty row of stools at the bar. I shrug off my coat and drape it over the chair next to me and place my purse on the seat.

"This isn't your normal seat. And where's the rest of the girl gang?" Jake's deep voice greets me.

"Just me today and it's mostly business."

"And what kind of business would that be?" Jake rests both his palms on the bar, leaning forward and locking his elbows like he's about to do a push-up.

"Well, you know, Seth and his family lost The Lilith House."

"Yeah, a fire. I heard about that on the news."

"I'm organizing a charity event and auction to help them recoup some of what they lost, and I was wondering if you would donate the use of Porter's for a night—"

"I'll do it."

"—so we could have a space to host the event."

"Parisa, I said I'll do it. You can have the bar for a night."

"Really? Just like that? I had an entire speech prepared about how this will be good for your business with the extra publicity."

"The bar is doing just fine. I don't need the publicity. But I like Seth. His family are caring and compassionate people. They deserve this. I'll even do you one better. We'll serve the alcohol because we all know money flows after a few drinks. And I'll donate half the drink profits."

"Are you for real? That's too much. I can't ask for that."

"You don't have to ask. I'm offering."

My lips pull into a giant smile. Everything is coming together better than I expected. I reach for my phone in my purse and open the notes app. I put a check next to Secure Venue and set my phone down. "I'm hoping everyone on my list will be this easy."

"Who else are you asking?"

"I have Bennett and Trey. I know they'll help but it's also asking them to ask some of their high-profile clients and friends to offer some gifts for the auction."

"Those two could schmooze a bear out of hibernation. They'll get shit done. What else?"

"I need a caterer who'll make hors d'oeuvres. Nothing

fancy. Just finger food to keep people around. Know anyone?"

"I might know someone. They owe me a favor. It won't be anything Michelin star, but I can guarantee it will be good."

"I'll take it! That's a better option than mine."

"Who do you have?"

"No one." I shrug my shoulders and Jake lets out a hearty laugh.

"Thank you so much Jake. But now that my work here is done. On to the next." I stand, grabbing my coat and tugging my arm through the hole before repeating the process with the other arm. "Also, do you happen to have a growler of the new oatmeal stout? A little liquid enticement should help Bennett agree to all this."

"Yeah. I'll grab you one."

Now that I can cross Jake off the list, Bennett and Trey are next. I know Charlie and Olivia were going to mention something, but I really want to make sure I can cross them off my list. Luckily for me, as soon as I pull into Bennett's driveway my headlights shine directly on Trey's black Escalade. Two birds with one stone. They can even share the growler.

I throw my car into park next to Trey's and hop out. I walk up the pathway and up the few steps until I'm on the porch of Bennett's two-story modern farmhouse. A motion light flickers to life, lighting the rest of my way. I knock on the wood door. The murmur of voices can be heard on the other side. But after a few seconds, no one answers, so I take off my mitten and knock again, this time a little harder. The porch is lit up when the front door opens and Bennett stands on the other side.

"Hi, Parisa. Come in. Let me get Charlie." Bennett steps out of the way and holds the door open for me as I walk through the doorway.

"Actually, I'm here to see you. And it's even better that Trey is here too."

"Parisa. I-I don't want to break your heart but I'm a happily taken man. But Trey on the other hand—"

I smack Bennett in the stomach with my purse and he doubles over with an oomph. "No, you idiot. I need to talk to you guys about a charity event for Seth. I brought you a growler but after that comment I might just keep it for myself." I hold up the sixty-four ounce glass jug.

"Since you brought beer..." Bennett grabs the bottle from my grasp and makes his way into the kitchen. I follow close behind, walking into the open kitchen where Charlie and Trey are sitting at the island. "I got beer and Parisa is here."

"Beer and a pretty lady. This night just got better." Trey stands up and greets me with a hug.

"Parisa. What are you doing here?" Charlie wraps her arms around me next. "Let me take your coat." She holds out her arms as I shrug it off.

"I was in the area so I thought I would stop by and talk to Bennett and Trey, since he's here, about the charity event." I take a seat at the end of the island.

Bennett removes four pint glasses from the cupboard and sets them on the concrete countertop. He opens the jug and starts pouring.

I wave him off. "I'm good."

"Do you want wine? I have a bottle of red." Charlie rises from her seat but sits back down when I respond.

"No, thanks. I'm here strictly for business."

"Oh, this is getting serious." Trey reaches for one of the full pints and takes a sip.

"Once I heard about all the trouble Seth and his family are having regarding The Lilith House, I knew I needed to do something. So, I'm putting together a charity event to help raise money. And I need your help."

"Charlie mentioned something, but what do you need our help with?" Bennett leans forward, resting his elbows on the counter.

"I'm hoping that you and Trey could talk to some of your friends and clients about donating some items to our silent auction."

Bennett's fingers brush across the dark stubble on his chin. "I think there are a few people I can ask. And a few others who owe me a favor. So yeah, I'll see what I can do."

"Same. Anything to help Seth and his family," Trey says.

"Oh Bennett, maybe you could donate one of the trestle tables you built. And matching chairs to go with it," Charlie adds.

"That's a great idea. Count me in for a dining set. It won't be done in time for the event, but it can be like an IOU."

"Everyone is going to love that. That will for sure bring in a lot of money." I pull out my phone and open the notes app to mark down Bennett's donation. "Also, let me know as soon as possible what your friends can donate. Or give them my number and I'll organize everything."

"Wow Parisa. I've never seen you like this. Hosting an event of this magnitude and making notes in your phone verses a cocktail napkin. What have you done with the other Parisa?" Charlie playfully bumps me with her elbow.

"Let's just say a certain bow tie wearing guy taught me the importance of being organized."

"Does he know you're doing all this?" Bennett asks.

"He doesn't and I hope to keep it a surprise. If all goes as planned, I hope to surprise him with an invitation to the event." I fiddle with my phone.

"You've always been so determined. I know you'll make this entire event amazing." Charlie leans over, giving me a side hug.

"I hope so."

"I got it!" Trey's booming voice startles us all.

"Got what?" Bennett asks.

"I have the perfect donation." Trey's smile lights up the kitchen.

"I'm scared to ask, but what do you got?" I ask.

"Me!"

"You?" I quirk an eyebrow at him.

"Yeah. The highest bidder wins a date with me." Trey sits up straighter and puffs out his chest, proud of his genius idea as if he just invented the wheel.

"You think that highly of yourself? That you'll bring in a bunch of cash?" Charlie asks.

"Hey, I'm a catch," Trey defends himself.

"I'm sure they'll catch something," I retort.

"That's a Seth comment. You've been hanging out with him too much." Trey points in my direction.

"You do realize prostitution is illegal, right?" I reply.

"I'm not going to have sex with them. Unless they want to pay extra." Trey winks.

I drop my head to my hands. I can't believe what I'm about to do and I pray I don't regret it. Lifting my head, I stare at Trey. "You know what. Fine. We'll auction you off."

"Yes!" Trey fist pumps the air. "But it has to be one of those live auctions."

The next day I walk into The Blue Stone Group like a woman on a mission. Because this is the biggest thing I've ever done, and I hope I'm not ignored. I stride past the reception desk, offering a quick wave to Olivia as she gives me a fierce smile. My heart hammers in my chest because what if they say no? Then I will have to go to plan B. Only I have no plan B.

Once I'm at the elevator I press the up arrow and it lights up. A few seconds later, the doors open. I walk inside and as soon as I turn around the doors close. I let out a deep breath and press the button for the third floor. For the entire ride up to my floor I count the heartbeats thumping in my throat. When the doors open, I quickly drop off my belongings at my desk and hurry to Mr. Evans' office. My heart is racing as sweat collects on my palms, but I need to do this. This is no longer about me, but for the community and a family who wants to serve them.

Through the slits in the vertical blinds, I see he's sitting behind his desk. The door is open a crack when I arrive. I take a deep breath, hoping to calm my erratic nerves, but it doesn't help. It's now or never. I raise my hand and softly knock before peeking my head through the opening.

"Mr. Evans, do you have a moment so I can speak with you?"

He looks up from the paperwork sitting on his desk. "Parisa. Yes, come in. Take a seat."

Pushing the door open, I slide inside and close the door behind me with a click. With confident strides, I make my way to the leather armchair sitting in front of Mr. Evans' desk.

"What can I help you with today?" Mr. Evans intertwines his fingers and rests them on top of his paperwork.

I place the folder on my lap and mimic his actions. "It's been mentioned that The Blue Stone Group has been in some hot water with the community over the removal of a community park caused by one of our developments. And I believe I have a solution to get the community back on our side."

He drops his hands. "And what's that?"

"Recently, a vitally important asset to our community has been lost because of a fire. The Lilith House."

"I heard about that. But where does The Blue Stone Group come in?"

Opening the folder on my lap, I place a few papers in front of Mr. Evans. "I know The Blue Stone Group has recently purchased a lot, downtown, that has a few buildings onsite. At this moment, there are no plans in motion for the use of that lot. I believe it would make a prime location for The Lilith House to rebuild."

"And we sell that lot to The Lilith House?"

"I believe if The Blue Stone Group donated the lot to The Lilith House, the people would see how the company wants to help the community instead of destroying it."

"I see what you're saying. That is a big donation to be making and a lot of lost revenue for the company."

"I understand, but we should think long term. And having The Blue Stone Group involved in such a pivotal asset to the community will help bring the residents back to our side." I flip through a few more pages of my papers and pull out two more and hand them to Mr. Evans. "These are the numbers of how many people The Lilith

House has helped." Pointing to another graph on the paper, I add, "And these are the numbers of how many people The Lilith House has transitioned back into the community by providing food, shelter, and even finding employment. And even more, believing in them."

Mr. Evans leans back in his chair. "I see you've done your research. You do offer a compelling case. I will have to discuss this with the CEO and get back to you with a final decision."

"That's all I can ask for. Thank you, Mr. Evans."

I rise to my feet and straighten my blouse. I turn on my heel not feeling defeated but not entirely confident either. All I can do is cross my fingers.

chapter twenty-seven
Peach Cobbler, You're Favorite

Seth

The drive through the snow is brutal today. My hands grip the steering wheel a little tighter. I had no intention of leaving my house, but my mom called and told me I'm needed at their house. They discharged her from the hospital after a week's stay. They couldn't find anything that was a definite cause of the heart attack, but told her to take it easy for a while just in case. Every possible scenario of what it could be runs through my mind. Has her health worsened? Did they find out the cause of the fire?

As I come up on my parents' driveway, I push down on the brake pedal, but my tires lock up and slide. The ABS kicks in, but my car just slides and slides. Once I come to a stop about ten feet past the driveway, I shift into reverse before taking the right turn following the path of previous tire tracks. I park in front of the garage and stroll up to the front door, letting myself in.

Once in the foyer I untie my shoes and place them next to the bench with the other shoes and hang up my jacket on the coat rack. Suddenly, I'm assaulted with a sweet, sugary aroma. Fucking hell. Strolling into the kitchen, Mom has an apron tied around her waist while my dad and sister sit at the kitchen island enjoying whatever Mom has just baked.

"Smells good in here." I greet my mom with a side hug. I didn't want to be rude, but I didn't know what else to say since this scent does things to me and I'm hoping those things stay at bay.

"Thanks, honey. I was told to relax and baking helps me do that. Plus, your sister gave me this peach cobbler recipe. She said it was your favorite."

My gaze darts to Bri as she shoves a large bite of cobbler into her mouth. "Mmm. This is good," she mumbles around a mouth full of peaches and crumble.

"Sit down. I'll get you a piece." Mom directs me to the empty seat next to Bri and grabs a small plate from the cupboard. She scoops up a still warm piece and places it in front of me.

I dig my fork in and take a bite. It's sweet and delectable, just like *her*. But I'd pick her over this cobbler any day.

Wanting to cut to the chase, I ask, "So what did you need to talk about? Any health news? Did they find anything about the fire?"

"To answer all your questions, no new health news. We heard about the fire. Apparently, it originated in the basement and by the time it spread to the main floor it was so big it was hard to control. But the cause of the fire is inconclusive."

"What does that mean with the insurance?"

"We'll get some insurance money."

"But not enough to pay for a new building." My fork drops to the plate with a clatter.

"No. It won't. But this came in the mail today." Mom slides a square, stamped envelope in my direction.

Flipping it over, I open the already broken flap and pull out two items. I turn over the thick cardstock. I gloss over the script text.

"What is this?" I hold up the paper.

"It's an invitation for a charity event. To raise money for The Lilith House."

My eyebrows knit together, confusion covering my face. "Did you organize this?"

Mom shakes her head and points to the other paper. "Read that."

Unfolding the other paper, I scan the words. Holy shit. My gaze darts up to meet Mom's. A beaming smile covers her face.

"The Blue Stone Group has donated a building to The Lilith House. We don't need to worry about a new building. And that…" Mom points to the cardstock paper, "is an invitation for a charity auction to help raise money for additional funding we may need."

"That's so amazing, Mom," Bri exclaims. "Isn't that wonderful Seth?"

I stare down at the two papers again in disbelief. "Yeah. It is." But I don't understand why The Blue Stone Group would do all this for me and my family after my sudden departure.

Later that night on my way home I decide to swing by Bennett's house since it's on the way. When I pull into his driveway, a soft glow shines from the large picture window informing me someone's home. Putting my car into park, I climb out and walk up the shoveled sidewalk until I reach the porch. Before I can raise my hand to knock the door opens, a large shadow fills the frame.

"Hey, man. Saw you drive up. Come on in." Bennett moves out of the doorway, and I step past him. "What brings you here?"

I remove my shoes and jacket and follow him into the living room. Charlie is sitting cross legged on the couch knitting something. Bennett takes a seat next to her and I sit in a recliner opposite them. "I was at my parents' house, and they got something interesting in the mail. What do you know about a charity auction for The Lilith House?"

Bennett leans forward, resting his elbows on his knees. "Oh, about that—"

"That was all Parisa," Charlie interrupts.

"What do you mean?"

Charlie sets her knitting needles on the couch cushion. "Parisa set that up. She convinced The Blue Stone Group to donate the building and she's been working tirelessly day and night on arranging everything from the location, food, and auction items."

My chest tightens. I stare straight ahead, forgetting to blink. Parisa did all this. I can't believe it.

"We all called in some favors to help raise as much money as possible. We all know how much The Lilith House means to you and your family," Bennett says.

"Wow. I don't know what to say. Thank you."

"Don't thank us. It was all Parisa's idea." Bennett leans back on the couch and crosses his leg over his knee.

"She really cares for you. She knows she made some

mistakes and now she's trying to right those mistakes." Charlie leans forward to look at me.

For the next hour, I tell Bennett and Charlie about the cause of the fire being inconclusive, my mom's health, and how I'll be working at The Lilith House now. But the entire time my thoughts are on Parisa. And now armed with this new information, I'm more confused than ever.

chapter twenty-eight
Nana Wins A Date

Seth

I hold the door open to Porter's, a chill sweeps through the air as my mom and dad step through and I follow close behind. Snowflakes litter my jacket. I take a moment to brush them off before looking up and my jaw drops. This place doesn't look like the Porter's I'm used to. All the pub tables are moved to sit in front of the small stage. Candles sit in the middle as centerpieces. On the far wall, various items sit on top of tables as people stroll along the rows.

Several groups of people are gathered around various tables while waiters and waitresses walk around with trays of appetizers. Behind the bar Jake and a couple of other bartenders serve drinks to thirsty patrons. My parents walk off to greet some friends and I'm left all alone. I scan the room in hopes I'll find Parisa.

"Here man, you look like you could use this." Bennett comes up next to me with Charlie and hands me a beer.

"Thanks." I take the beer from him and swallow a big gulp, shock still coursing through my body.

Olivia and Hollyn join us with drinks and cupcakes.

"This Almond Joy cupcake is to die for." Olivia takes another bite, her eyes closing as she savors the taste. "Seriously, Hollyn you outdid yourself with these."

"Thanks, Hollyn for making all the cupcakes. It means a lot to me and my parents," I say.

"I'm happy I could help. And the plus side, I've booked a couple parties with how much people have loved them. So, win-win." A wide smile covers Hollyn's face.

Parisa and Trey stroll up to us arguing about when they'll start the date auction.

Trey screeches to a halt. His gaze darts to Hollyn then to Parisa. "Wait, there are two of you? Why did no one tell me?"

"Trey, this is my sister Hollyn. Hollyn, Trey." Parisa points between the two.

Trey steps into the middle of our small circle until he's standing in front of Hollyn with his hand held out. "Hi Hollyn, I'm Trey. Whatever they told you about me is probably true, but you should really find out for yourself."

Before Hollyn can place her hand in his, Parisa is gripping the collar of his shirt and tugging him back. "Oh no. No. No. No. Stay away from my sister, or I'll cut off your nuts and duct tape them to your face."

Trey holds up his hands like he's surrendering. "I'll stay away from her, but I can't guarantee she'll stay away from me." He winks at Hollyn. Parisa jolts toward him and instantly his hands move to cover his nuts. "Violence is not the answer."

"Ugh. Let's just get this auction thing figured out." Parisa grabs Trey's wrist and drags him toward the stage.

Charlie rises to her tippy toes and presses a kiss onto Bennett's cheek before she scampers off to talk to someone she knows, along with Hollyn and Olivia. Bennett's eyes are fixated on Charlie's every move the whole time, until she's on the other side of the room, adoration flashes across his face.

"So how did you know?" I ask.

Bennett's gaze drifts from Charlie to me. "Know what?"

"How did you know Charlie was the one?"

"It had to be the moment when she invaded every waking, and every sleeping, moment of my time. She's a little piece of me that makes me whole. A piece I never knew I was missing."

I nod at his words. Everything he said is exactly how I feel about Parisa. She's the little missing piece in my life that I need to make me whole, but fuck, I don't know how to make her see that. From the first time our lips touched she set my soul on fire, burning bigger and brighter every time she's near. But stolen kisses only last for so long.

Charlie motions Bennett to where she's standing with a group of people. While he walks to her, I use that time to inspect all the silent auction items. There is everything from discounts on repairs services, vacation rentals, high end recreation coolers, and clubhouse seats to baseball games. I continue walking down the table when I see a picture of a trestle table donated by Bennett and Charlie. A wide grin covers my face knowing I have some of the best friends a guy could ask for. But the next item on the table makes my heart drop. Sandwiched between the picture of the Bennett's table and a gift basket, sits three black framed photographs. The first is of the sea smoke over Lake Superior. The next one is of the gazebo at Bristol Beach, and the last one featuring a lighthouse sitting next to the rising sun. I look down to the place card that reads:

Donated by Parisa Anthony

I scribble down my bid and continue down the line to look at all the other items until a familiar voice pours through the speakers. Turning around, Parisa is standing in the middle of the stage, a spotlight shining down on her causing her light pink sequined dress to sparkle. Her auburn hair is curled and drapes over her right shoulder.

"Thank you everyone for joining us tonight. I'm so happy so many people could come out and support The Lilith House. We have a very special treat for you, but first, be sure to grab a drink from the bar. Porter's has very graciously volunteered to donate half the drink proceeds to The Lilith House, so the more you drink the more we raise." Chuckles float through the crowd. "Also, if you haven't checked it out, we have rows of tables filled with silent auction items—" Parisa's gaze drifts my way and the moment our eyes connect she freezes. A small smile plays on my lips, and she reciprocates before she continues. "So be sure to jot down your bid. We'll announce the winners later this evening. You don't need to be present to win. So without further ado, mostly because he's antsy and won't stop bouncing on his toes." Laughs and chuckles come from the crowd. "Win a date with this handsome hunk." Parisa does a Vanna White arm wave as Trey struts out to the middle of the stage. And for good measure, he does a twirl to show off all his angles.

"Alright ladies and perhaps even gents, all are welcome. It's time to get those dollars out and start bidding. You can win a one-night date with Trey." Parisa points in Trey's direction and he does his best model strut as he makes his way from one side of the stage to the other. Catcalls and whistles sound from the crowd when Trey flashes them his boyish grin. "He's funny, and charming, and will make you laugh." That gets another round of hoots and hollers from the crowd. "He's housebroken… maybe. I can't make any guarantees—"

Trey grabs the mic from Parisa. "No need to worry about that, ladies." Another eruption of claps and whistles come from the crowd.

"House broken is up for debate but he's tall. I'm sure he'd be good at replacing a light bulb. Maybe carry some groceries." Trey stands off to the side flexing his muscles under his button-down shirt.

"Alright ladies, do I need to say more? Let's start the bidding at one hundred dollars!" Parisa rambles a bunch of words like an auctioneer, but no one can understand what she's actually saying.

Someone in the crowd raises their hand. "We have one hundred. Who's got one fifty." Hands ping pong throughout the crowd. "Two hundred. Two fifty." More hands raise in the crowd. "Three hundred." To three fifty then four. The bidding keeps increasing to four fifty and then five. Suddenly someone in the crowd shouts out one thousand. And the crowd goes silent.

"Wow. One thousand dollars going once. Going twice. Sold to the brunette in the red dress! I don't have a gavel…" Parisa then taps the top of the mic sending a thud sound through the speakers. The crowd erupts in claps and cheers.

Parisa and Trey step off the stage and walk their way through the crowd. I make my way toward them along with Charlie and Bennett. We all meet toward the back between the stage and the bar. I run into Parisa first. Not knowing what to say, I offer her a hi. Then I mentally slap myself.

She looks up at me. "Hi." Her voice is quiet and breathy.

"Maybe we can—"

Trey comes up behind me and clasps my shoulder. "Well, look at that. Someone paid one thousand dollars for a date with me." We all burst out laughing.

"Trey, you were right. You brought in a lot of money with your donation," Parisa says.

"Let's meet the lucky lady." Trey rubs his hands together in anticipation.

Parisa finds the girl with the winning bid and brings her to Trey. She's an attractive girl. Brown, curly hair that hangs past her shoulders. Petite frame. "Trey, this is Jenna. Jenna, this is Trey."

Trey holds out his hand and she places hers in his. He brings her hand up and presses a kiss to the top of her hand. "Jenna, you're a wise woman, you bid on the right item tonight. Should we go and get this date started right now?"

Jenna giggles before she pulls her hand from his. "Actually, the bid wasn't for me."

"Oh, you have a friend." Trey scans the room with hopes in finding who the friend is.

"The bid was for my Nana." Jenna turns around and grabs an older lady with short, curly white hair and brings her into our small circle. "Her senior living facility is having a Seniors Prom and Nana didn't have a date, so we thought this would be perfect. She'll be all everyone talks about if she brings a strapping young man like yourself."

All of us try to bite back our laughter. Charlie coughs from her drink and I turn my head hoping to hide my grin. Trey narrows his eyes as he stares down each and every one of us.

Trey wraps his arm around Nana. "Well Nana, it would be my pleasure to take you to prom. But get your dancing shoes ready because it will be a night you'll never forget."

Nana beams up at Trey, some of her red lipstick smeared on her too white to be real teeth and we can't help but cheer and clap for Nana. While everyone is preoccupied, I grasp Parisa's elbow to get her attention.

"Do you have a min—"

"Parisa, we need your help in the kitchen," a waitress interrupts.

"Of course. I'll be right there." Parisa sends the waitress on her way and turns back to me. "Can you give me a minute?"

"Certainly." I nod and watch her every step as she follows the waitress' path through the steel double doors into the kitchen.

Once our small crowd disperses, Trey comes and stands next to me. "You know she still wants to wrap herself up in your bow ties and offer herself as a present to you."

"How do you know?"

"A girl would never go to these lengths for a guy she just tolerates." I ponder his words for a few seconds. "Plus, her eyes scream 'fuck me, Seth, fuck me.'"

When I turn toward him, a wide grin covers his face. I can't help but shake my head, while a smile of my own tugs at my lips. "I thought maybe you'd grown up a little bit until that last comment."

Trey clasps me on my shoulder. "Gotta keep you on your toes. I'm going to go find Jenna to make sure I can't convince her to take that date with me."

On that note, he's off meandering through the crowd. The music quiets down and I look up as Parisa takes the stage.

chapter twenty-nine
You Picked Me

Parisa

As soon as my heels hit the stage the music dies down. The sound of whispers and murmurs carry around the large, open space along with the thumping of my heartbeat. As soon as I grab the microphone, a spotlight shines down on me. Raising my hand, I shield my eyes as they adjust to the blinding light. I've spent so much time thinking about myself and after everything that happened with Seth and The Lilith House, I knew all of this was bigger than me. And Seth deserves more than what I've given him. And now is my time to show him.

I lift the microphone to my mouth. "I-I would like to thank everyone who came out tonight and supported this fundraiser." I shift my weight back and forth. "A big thank you to The Blue Stone Group for their generosity in helping The Lilith House and everyone who donated items for the auction. Of course, thank you to Jake for allowing us to use his bar to host the event and The Sweet Spot for providing desserts." I pause to take a deep breath while everyone claps. "The Lilith House is such an important staple in our community. They do so much for other people, so I'm grateful we could all come together to help them. And I know all the money raised tonight will go on to help so many individuals and families."

My eyes scan the room. I spot Bennett and Charlie standing with Trey and Olivia. Then my sister. My breath hitches when I see Seth. My heart hammers in my chest, but I continue. "When something goes wrong, everyone deserves a second chance. The Lilith House deserves a second chance. But also, people deserve a second chance. Like me. I messed up a great opportunity with an amazing guy because I was scared. And let me tell you, nothing sucks more than losing the one thing you care about most. I let my own fears and insecurities get in the way of something I know would be magical. Because he is the one person who always makes me feel special. Like I was the only one in a room." My feet carry me from one side of the stage to the other. "And now I'm rambling."

Heads shift from left to right as hushed voices carry around the room. I stop, my gaze fixates on only one person and he's staring back at me, his expression stoic. So, I make one last ditch effort. To let him know I'm all in. All I want is him. He's all I ever wanted. My heart knew that the first time we kissed. "All I want is a second chance to make everything right. But most of all, I'm sorry." He stands there motionless, as if he's a statue, his expression blank.

My hand holding the microphone drops to my side as my gaze casts downward, feeling defeated. After what feels like hours, the sound of a single person clapping echoes in the quiet room. Then a second clap, a third, and a fourth. Soon enough, the entire room is clapping.

When I glance up, Seth is storming up the stairs to the stage. I turn toward him, his face still expressionless. Once he's a few short strides from me, the corners of his lips tip up into a smile. Within seconds, his hands clutch my cheeks as his lips collide with mine. It's a kiss laced with fury and passion. Months of emotions spill out of us in this one moment. The roar of the crowd below us diminishes as my only thoughts are of Seth. The microphone tumbles from my grip and drops to the stage with a clatter. My arms wrap around Seth's neck until I'm threading my fingers through his soft locks. I never want to let him go.

Slowly, Seth breaks the kiss but doesn't lessen his grip. "You know, you can't hide this anymore because everyone just saw us kiss."

Heat blasts across my chest and up to my cheeks when realization hits me that everyone just witnessed that kiss. But I don't care anymore. I press my swollen lips together until I can't hide the smile that covers my face and I look up into his bright green eyes. "Good, because I want everyone to know that you picked me." Seth's eyes glint before his lips tip up into a smile. Within seconds, his lips are on mine again, but this kiss is much quicker.

More hoots and hollers from the crowd pull us from our tender moment. Seth removes his hands from my cheeks and wraps one around my waist, holding me tight. We both turn toward the crowd and Seth bends down to pick up the microphone. He waves his hand holding the mic in the air and the crowd quiets down. He looks down at me before turning and addressing everyone.

"From me and my family I want to personally thank everyone for making this such an amazing event. We were devastated when we got the news that The Lilith House burned down. To have a community that rallied around us is an amazing feeling. And I have to thank Parisa for putting all this together. I have no words besides thank you."

I look up to Seth while he looks down at me, a tear pricks the corner of his eye and I give him a small smile.

His arm still wrapped around my waist squeezes me before he turns back toward the crowd. "And Parisa is right, everyone deserves a second chance and I'm so thankful The Lilith House gets theirs. But now, if you'll excuse us, we have some other unfinished business to attend to."

The crowd erupts again with a mix of clapping, whistling, and catcalls. Followed by someone yelling *Hell yeah you do*, which I can only assume is Trey. Seth lets go of my waist and grabs my hand. He tugs me along as he places the microphone back on the stand and drags me off the stage, happy to go wherever he goes.

chapter thirty
About Damn Time

Seth

"We are not having sex in the bathroom of Porter's again." Parisa puts her heel into the floor jolting me back.

"Well shit. Where do we go then?" My eyes dart left and then right, finding the perfect spot. "Follow me." Several feet down the hallway, we come to a partially closed door with a sign that reads Office hanging on the front. I push the door open and flick the light switch. The harsh florescent lights shine down almost killing the mood. Almost.

Once Parisa's inside, I shut the door and lock it. When I turn around, she's watching my every move, a smile playing on her lips. She saunters up to me. The palms of her hands roam up my torso, across my chest, then she's tugging on the straps of my suspenders. Her lips are mere inches away from mine. Lust fills her hazel eyes.

"So, you got me here, what are you going to do with me?" Her fingers play with the buttons on my shirt.

"I'm going to make this second chance count. Now, take off your dress."

I take a step back and quickly take in my surroundings. There's not much besides a desk and a few filing cabinets that line the back wall. I can work with a desk.

Parisa reaches behind her and slowly slides the zipper down. I sidestep her while she undresses and begin moving the papers on the desk into neat piles and setting them off to the side.

"What are you doing? Are you cleaning Jake's desk?"

"Look, it's not my stuff. I don't know if it's important, so I don't want to just throw it on the floor and cause a mess."

"Seth, look at me."

I glance over my shoulder, Parisa is standing there, her arms hugging her chest holding her dress up. Then she drops her arms, the dress cascades down her body and pools at her feet. Slowly, I turn around taking in the sight before me. She's wearing nothing but a black silk thong and black heels. My gaze travels up her thighs, over her hips, and up her torso to her bare chest. The tips of her wavy auburn hair lays right above her hard, dusty rose nipples. Finally, my gaze stops on her beautiful oval face, and her plump lips that she's currently nibbling on. I reach down and adjust my aching cock. "

Now, you have five seconds to decide what you're going to do before I lift that dress back up and walk out of here. What's it going to be?"

"Sorry Jake," I mumble to myself.

I make a mental note to tell him I'll clean it up later.

With one swipe of my arm, I'm clearing everything off his desk. Papers flutter to the floor around me. I turn back around and in a few quick strides, I'm standing in front of her. Resting my hands on her hips, I turn her around and push her backward. Once the back of her thighs hit the edge of the desk, I lift her up, and she lets out a squeak as I set her on the desktop. With my palms splayed on top of the cool wood desk, I cage her in.

Leaning in, I brush my nose against hers, breathing in her peach scent. "You make me do things I don't want to do. But for you, I'll do them."

As soon as the words leave my mouth, her lips are on mine. Her hands skate up my forearms and across my biceps until she reaches my shoulders. Then swiftly she's tugging down my suspenders. I move my arms so the straps fall to my sides. With our lips still fused together, she makes quick work of removing my bow tie and unbuttoning my shirt. She breaks our kiss for a brief moment once she reaches the waistband of my pants and I help her with the process. I fumble to release the button of my slacks as a mixture of nerves and excitement course through my body. Once they're undone, they fall to my feet. Parisa peels my shirt from my shoulders, down my arms, until it drops to the floor. My hands run up her thighs as goosebumps cover her skin. Once I reach her waist, I tug her forward so she's right on the edge of the desk. I bring my hands to the front of her and trail a finger down her slit. Her head falls back, and she spreads her legs wider.

"I've barely even touched you and you're already so wet for me." I rub circles on her clit, applying a little more pressure each turn.

"Seth. Shit. That feels so good."

I run my finger down through her wetness until I find her opening. Slowly, I slide my finger inside. Past one knuckle, then stop when I reach the second. A moan escapes Parisa's lips as I pull my finger out and repeat the motion. Her hips slowly buck into my hand, like she wants more so I give it to her. When I pull my finger out, I plunge back in adding a second finger. After a few pumps in and out, I add a third. I bend down and swirl my tongue around her erect nipple before sucking it into my mouth. Parisa brings her hand up, fingers combing my hair at the back of my head.

"Oh, Seth! Don't stop! I'm going to come!" Parisa's moans grow louder with each pump of my fingers.

I bite down on her nipple, and she explodes. Her pussy contracts around my fingers as she rides out her orgasm. Her hand that was in my hair flies to her mouth as she attempts to muffle her moans. I pull my fingers out, her orgasm glistens on my fingers. With hooded eyes, she watches as I bring them up to my mouth and suck off her wetness. The taste of her makes my cock even harder, if that was possible. Reaching down, I grab my throbbing dick and rub the swollen head up and down her slit. Parisa sits up to watch. Before I push into her it, hits me.

"Fuck. I don't have a condom. Why do we always end up like this?" I rest my forehead against hers.

"Oh." She's silent for a moment before speaking, "You can pull out."

"You're not worried about getting pregnant?"

"You are the only guy I want to be with. So, if it happens, it happens." Her bright, doe-like eyes meet mine.

Parisa pregnant with my child... Something about that vision puts a smile on my face. "Fuck. I love you."

"I love you. But it's been way too long. So shut up and stick your cock in me."

"You know what happens when you make demands?"

"That's why I said it." A sly smile graces her lips.

Gripping her hips, I pull her off the desk and turn her around. My left hand grips the back of her neck and pushes down. She knows exactly what I'm about to do to her and she willingly bends forward until her cheek is resting on the desk. She wiggles her round, plump ass just to tempt me. With my hand still gripping her neck, I pull my right hand back and, like a rubber band I snap it forward until it connects with her pale skin. Parisa lets out a soft yelp, but it quickly turns into a moan while I massage the reddening skin.

"You look so hot like this. You want another?"

"Mmm yes."

"Good girl."

I release my left hand from her neck and bring it back to deliver another smack on her ass, but this time on the opposite side. Another moan escapes her.

"Let's see how wet you are for me." I slide a finger down the crack of her ass until I reach her pussy. At first, I swirl the pad of my finger around in her honey before I plunge inside of her.

"Oh yes! More!" Her words are breathy.

"Like this?" I add a second finger, pumping in and out.

"Oh fuck! Just like that."

"How about this?" Using my hands, I spread her open from behind. I dip down, running my tongue between her cheeks until I find her clit. I lap at her sweet arousal coating my tongue. Her body writhes above me.

"Oh yes! Seth! That feels so good." Her horse words spur me on more.

I continue alternating between flicking and swirling my tongue around her clit. I push a finger inside her with a hook motion, hitting her G spot, her pussy spasms around my finger. Her wetness coats my finger as I pull out. I bring it up to my lips and suck it all off.

"I've never tasted anything better. But just so you know, I'm not done with you." I rise to my feet and Parisa rises as well, but I stop her. "Where do you think you're going? I want you just like this." I grab both her wrists and bring them to the small of her back. Using one hand, I hold her wrists behind her. Reaching for my bow tie on top of the desk, I wrap it around her wrists in a figure eight motion and I clutch the two ends in my hand. "Let me know if this gets too tight. I had to improvise with just one bow tie, and I don't have much slack."

Before she can respond, I align myself with her entrance and thrust into her. A moan falls from her lips and I'm half tempted to find something to shove in her mouth to keep her quiet, but I love the sounds she makes. I pull the bow tie, causing her to arch her back, and a deep moan leaves her throat as I drive into her. Harder. Faster. Between my thrusts and her weight pushing forward, the desk begins to shift. Each thrust causing it to creak forward.

My pace quickens as Parisa's moans get louder. Her pussy contracts around my dick, sending a bolt of pleasure coursing through my body. I bend down and place a kiss on the back of her neck. She is everything I didn't know I needed in my life. The chaos to my structure. The wild to my calm. And I never want to lose her again. I want to claim her as mine. I want everyone to know she's mine. At that thought, my thrusts become more frantic, each one harder than the last.

"Fuck. Feeling you bare against my dick, I'm not going to last much longer." A tingle starts at the base of my spine just as Parisa's pussy clenches around my cock like a vise grip. My name tumbles off her lips and that's my undoing. Gripping my cock, I pull out and with a few more strokes I'm shooting my load onto her lower back and a little drips down the crack of her ass. I'm half tempted to smear my cum down to her pussy. Mix my orgasm with hers. But I'll save that for another time. I unwrap my bow tie from her wrists and they tumble to her sides. I think I wore my girl out. Quickly, I find a box of tissues and work on cleaning her up and then dispose of them in the trash can next to the desk.

Once I'm done, I pull her into my arms. Brushing a lock of hair from her eye, I tuck it behind her ear so I can get a full view of her beautiful face. Bright hazel eyes look up into mine. "I love you, Peach."

"I love you too." She rises onto her tippy toes and presses her lips to mine. Soft and sensual. Something I will never grow tired of. "We better get back out there before they think we're going for round two."

"Give me five minutes and there could be a round two." She playfully slaps my chest before bending down to collect her dress while I also get dressed.

Glancing over at Jake's desk, I cringe at the state of disarray we left it in. I tidy up the papers and move the desk back into position. When I turn around Parisa has her dress pulled up but peers at me over her shoulder. "Can you help me?" She nods at her open dress.

I stroll over to her and grab the zipper. Tugging up, I drag my finger over her soft skin. Goosebumps creep up her arms and her shoulders twitch. When the zipper reaches the top, I press a kiss to the back of her neck.

"What do you say? Shall we go get the third degree from our friends?"

She laces her fingers with mine. "Let's do this."

When we stroll out of Jake's office and back into the main area, the charity event is still in full swing. Charlie notices us first. Her gaze dips to our linked hands then back up with a face splitting grin. As we approach the high-top table where everyone is gathered, Bennett is the next to look our way and then Trey, followed by Olivia and Hollyn.

Trey's the first to break the silence. "It's about damn time."

"What do you mean 'about damn time'?" I ask.

"You two tried to hide your hook ups but we've known." Charlie takes a sip of her drink.

I glance around the table as everyone nods their heads like a gang of bobble heads sitting on a dashboard. "How long have you guys known? And why did no one say anything?"

"We wanted you guys to come to us when you were ready, but don't worry we've all discussed this among ourselves," Olivia says with a wink.

"I had my suspicions the night at Porter's when I saw Seth go off with a girl with a shiny thing in her hair. Then afterward you sat down at our table with the same shiny thing." Trey points to Parisa.

"So, a hair clip gave me away? I thought maybe it was our uncontrollable laughter when you mentioned the out of order sign on the men's bathroom door."

Trey's eyebrows pinch together. "Why? Wait. You put the sign there?"

Parisa and I laugh once again.

"Son of a bitch." Trey slaps the table. "I had to risk my life because you two were fucking in the bathroom. But also…that's genius. Where can I get one of those signs?"

"I found out at my farewell party from The Blue Stone Group. There was so much leg groping happening under the table," Charlie says.

"That's when Trey mentioned the hair clip. We all had a lengthy discussion after that," Bennett adds.

I wrap my arms around Parisa's waist, and she nuzzles into my chest. "We need to practice being stealthier."

Parisa peers up at me. "Or not, since everyone knows now."

"But you have to admit it was pretty fun." I squeeze her tighter to me and she wraps her arms around my waist.

Never in my wildest dreams would I have expected the one woman who infuriated me on a daily basis would also be the one woman I don't want to spend a single day without.

epilogue
Six Months Later

Parisa

I toss the paint roller onto the tray and wipe the sweat from my forehead with the back of my hand. Seth comes up to me and wraps his arm around my shoulder. "Looks good in here. If we hang a mirror on that wall. Then move the desk to the right about two feet. That would be a perfect spot for me to bend you over—"

Playfully, I backhand him in the stomach. "We are not having sex in the office of The Lilith House."

After the charity auction and getting all the legal paperwork taken care of, The Lilith House was the proud new owner of a new to us building. With Seth's mom still on the mend, he told his parents he would take control of all the contractors. I put my foot down when it came time to purchase a new dishwasher. They were getting the best of the best because I wasn't cleaning up water again.

Luckily, The Lilith House was able to use two different community centers to act as a temporary dinner hall while preparations were underway for the new location. Seth bossing people around is hot, and not just when he's doing it to me. Many nights I showed him just how hot it was, but of course, more times than not it ended with my wrists tied up with bow ties. After months of work, The Lilith House is only weeks away from the grand re-opening.

"Alright, no office sex… today." Seth flashes me a boyish grin. I can't help but smile in return.

I wander the perimeter of the room until I'm standing in front of three framed photos perched in the corner. "I still can't believe you got into a bidding war with my sister over the photos I took. I would have happily given both of you copies."

"It was worth every penny to have the originals. Plus, I knew they would make a great addition to the office." Seth moves to stand next to me.

"They look perfect in here." I smile up at Seth. Then my gaze drifts to my bag and my heart rate spikes. I've come to the conclusion there's no perfect time to share news like this. The perfect moment is the one we make. And there's no better moment then now. "I have something for you."

"You've changed your mind about the office sex?"

"You're insatiable. And no." I stroll to my bag and pull out a white pastry box with The Sweet Spot logo stamped on the top. "This is for you." With a slight tremble, I hold out the box to him. It feels like a swarm of butterflies are about to take flight in my stomach.

Seth eyes the box and then looks up at me. "What is this?"

"Just open it." I nibble on my lip in anticipation.

Seth slowly peels back the lid and peeks inside. With wide eyes, he looks up at me and back into the box. "Is this real?" All I can do is eagerly nod my head.

He reaches into the box and pulls out a frosted cupcake and resting on top is a pregnancy test with two pink lines. Seth lifts the cupcake to eye level as he inspects the test and pokes it. "No, is this real?"

I can't help the giggle that escapes. "No. The test is made of fondant. But what it shows is real."

"You're pregnant?"

I nod.

"We're having a baby?"

I nod again.

Seth sets the cupcake on the desktop and wraps his arms around my waist and lifts me. "We're going to have a baby Peach." His eyes light up as the biggest grin spreads across his face. "I love you so much."

"I love you." I press my lips to his. "Turns out, pulling out only works so long before it doesn't. Who knew?" I release a chuckle. If my dates are correct, it was the weekend after he had me bent over my dining room table. I told Seth I just got new neighbors and I should introduce him to them. Let's just say, Seth really enjoys when I get new neighbors.

"Who are we telling first?"

"Hollyn wants us to stop by the shop. Since she knew about the surprise, she wanted to make her congratulations official."

"Then let's go. I can't wait to tell the world." Seth sets me to my feet and tugs my hand as he walks toward the exit, his excitement contagious.

Hollyn

I drag the washcloth over the last white linoleum tabletop. The soft glow of the neon The Sweet Spot sign hangs in the storefront window above me. I started working here as soon as I finished culinary school. I've always had a sweet tooth for anything… sweet. But my dreams of owning my own bakery were cut short, so I did the next best thing, manage one.

The bell above the door chimes, startling me. I whirl around to see my sister and Seth stroll in. Instantly, a wide smile forms on my lips. I toss the wash rag onto the table and wrap Parisa in a big hug. Pulling away, I hold her at arm's length and look down expecting to see a noticeable difference, but Parisa says it's only been about six weeks so there is no visible sign of a baby bump yet.

"Congratulations to the both of you. I'm so excited to be an auntie and spoil him or her with all the toys and treats imaginable."

"Thanks for keeping it a surprise. It was pretty entertaining watching Seth's face when he saw the fondant pregnancy test." Parisa looks up at Seth.

"It looked so real. You did a fantastic job."

"Thank you. I have to admit that was my first edible pregnancy test."

Parisa rests her hand on her belly. "Just imagine you could do a whole line of pregnancy announcement cupcakes. And gender reveals. I bet those would be a hit."

Just then Olivia barrels through the door, holding her phone out in front of her, talking to someone. "Hold on. I just walked into The Sweet Spot, and everyone's here." Olivia lifts her gaze. "I have Charlie on FaceTime, and she has some news." Olivia squeals with excitement as she turns her phone around. Charlie and Bennett come into view on the small screen.

"Hey everyone. So… this happened." Charlie holds up her left hand, a massive diamond taking up her ring finger. "We're getting married!" A collective round of cheers and congratulations makes its way around our group.

"Not wanting to steal Charlie's thunder but since we're all here… It's still early but…" Parisa looks up at Seth and he beams down at her. Then she rests a hand on her belly. Olivia notices first and her eyes go wide. "We're having a baby!" Parisa shouts. The Sweet Spot once again fills with excitement and cheers.

I'm hit with a slight pang of jealousy. My sister is having a baby, our friends are getting married, and then there's me. Single and alone. It's been so long since I've had sex, I think my vagina has shriveled up into itself. I've been on dates, but as each day passes, the pool of quality men to fish from gets smaller and smaller. Even friends who set me up with friends of friends turn out to be duds. Why is dating so hard? Not to mention, work takes up most of my time. But I've wallowed in enough self-pity. I plaster on a smile because I am genuinely excited for everyone's happy news. I was just expecting to be at a different point in my life by now.

Olivia directs the phone screen back on her. "You know what this means. We're having a party! There's a wedding and a baby coming, we're celebrating! Something big. It will be like a pre-bachelorette party for Charlie and a night out before your life is consumed with no sleep, baby vomit, and diapers for Parisa and Seth."

"So glad you could make that sound so enticing," Seth deadpans.

You can almost see the wheels turning while Olivia plans everything out in her head. Maybe a night out is what I need. Hell, I can't remember the last time I took a weekend off and just let loose. Leave all my cares and worries at home.

"Okay ladies, dust off your vaginas, well me and Hollyn," Olivia turns to Parisa, "because you get regular sex. I'm thinking we rent a limo and head to the Cities for a night of fun, laughter, and debauchery."

"Are you sure? We can do something small and intimate up here—"

Olivia cuts Parisa off. "Yes, I'm sure. We never did this while everyone was single, now everyone is pairing off so yes, it's happening. The guys can come too, and they can have their own guys night."

I think about Olivia's proposal. This is exactly what I need to get out of this rut. "I'm in!"

Olivia bounces back and forth on the balls of her stiletto heels in excitement. I make my way to the kitchen and pull out a box of miscellaneous cupcakes. When I return to the small seating area, I flip open the lid.

"I don't have champagne or anything for us, but I have cupcakes." Everyone reaches into the box and grabs a frosted cake. "Here's to Charlie and Bennett, Parisa and Seth, and our night of no inhibitions," I shout. We all toast with our cupcakes in the air.

Thank you so much for reading Flirting with the Enemy! If you want more Seth and Parisa, claim your copy of their fun and flirty bonus scene when you join my newsletter.

Hollyn's life is thrown into a tailspin when she discovers her younger, one-night stand is her new boss. One problem, a owning a bakery was never Van's dream. The race is on for Hollyn to convince him not the sell while he convinces her they should continue where they left off. As the days tick by, Hollyn finds it harder to resist the temptation. Pick up your copy of Flirting with the Stranger Today!

Continue reading for an excerpt of the next standalone book in the Harbor Highlands series, Flirting with the Stranger.

. . .

"Girl, get it!"

"Rip his shirt off!"

"Let's get to the good stuff!"

Voices yell around us, but I'm not sure who's saying what. Reluctantly, she rests her palm on mine. Her soft skin a contrast against my rough hand as her fingers wrap around mine. I'm half tempted to forget this party and take her behind the curtain. I shake the thought from my head. Instead, I hoist her out of the armchair and guide her to the chair in the middle of the room.

Once she's seated, I bend down again and whisper in her ear, "Is it okay if I touch you? Just on your hands and arms." Her gaze darts from me to her friends as if she wants them to give her an answer. Hoping to reassure her I add, "Because you can most definitely touch me."

Her eyes meet mine and she nods before choking out, "Yes."

That's all I need. I straddle her legs and swivel my hips. I grab her hand and run it under my shirt. Her warm fingertips drag across my skin. When she reaches the middle of my chest, I remove my hand, but she keeps hers there. Her fingertips roam down my chest, caressing every dip and valley of my abs as they dance with my movements. There's something hot and sensual with the way her fingers graze over my skin. I don't know what it is, but I don't want her to stop. When she reaches my waistband, she drops her hand to her lap. A pang of disappointment hits me from the loss of her touch. I love having her hands on me.

Then another idea pops into my head. Grabbing her hands, I take a step back, giving her enough room to stand in front of me. This time, I grab both of her hands and place them at the hem of my shirt. I bend down until I'm at the shell of her ear and whisper, "Take my shirt off."

Slowly, I lean back and study her face. Her forehead wrinkles, but her fingers continue to caress the hem of my shirt. She nibbles on her bottom lip, and I'm so tempted to take over and nibble it myself. I nod my head, encouraging her to continue. Her fingers grip the fabric and drag it up, exposing my heated skin to the cool air. Once she's removed my shirt as far as she can reach, I take over and pull it the rest of the way off. With one side of my shirt in one hand, I wrap it around her waist and grip the other end with my other hand and tug, causing her to press up against my chest. Electricity courses through me as I sway my hips back and forth against her body to the music.

Just as I find my grove, the song changes. The first few notes of "It's Gonna Be Me" by NSYNC blares through the speakers and I freeze. In fact, everyone in the room freezes. My gaze darts to the bartender. This song certainly wasn't on the playlist I gave her. All she does is give me a one shoulder shrug.

Never one to turn down a challenge, I turn my attention back to the girl in my arms and move my body to the beat.

The bombshell barks out a laugh. "You are not stripping to NSYNC."

"Oh, but I am. And I'm going to look good doing it, too." I flash her a sexy smirk.

At least the song has a beat I can work with. And offers plenty of opportunities to thrust my hips. Starting at my shoulders and down to my stomach, I roll my body like a slow-moving wave. At the end I thrust my hips and all the girls clap and cheer. Their encouragement spurs me on more. I bend at the knees, and dress be damned. I pick her up and wrap her legs around my waist. She gasps and rests her hands on my shoulders for support. Swiveling around, I peer over her shoulder and find what I need. Within a few steps I'm standing in front of the chair. I release her legs, and she slowly slides down my body. My dick rubs against her the entire way down. There's no way she can't tell how much she turns me on.

Once her feet are firmly planted on the floor, she flashes me a saucy smile. "I didn't know boy bands turned you on?"

Now it's my turn to laugh. "It's Justin. Though I prefer his solo career more." She chuckles. I love her laugh. It's soft and sweet and I want to spend the rest of the night making her laugh, amongst other things. With an arm wrapped around her waist, I tug her toward me so she's snug against my chest. "Actually, that's only for you. What do you say we get a drink after this?"

Her gaze droops to the floor. "I don't think that's a good idea."

"I think it's an excellent idea. Probably the best I've ever had." All I want is to spend more time with her and I'll do what I can to make that happen.

"Maybe you should give everyone else a dance." Her voice is so soft I almost don't hear her, but her fingertips lightly brush my bare chest.

"But what if I don't want to give anyone else a dance? You're the only one I want to dance with.

A few of the other girls woot and holler while another one screams out, "Rip his clothes off!"

"It sounds like your friends want you to rip my clothes off. I'd hate to disappoint them." I trail a finger down her flush cheek and she shivers from the contact. It's not just me who feels the chemistry radiating between us in waves. She wouldn't be this hesitant if she didn't feel it either. I can see it in her eyes. The way she brushes against me. The way her cheeks turn crimson from my touch.

"We paid you to dance for everyone, not just me." Her eyes shift back and forth, searching mine, waiting for my response.

As much as I don't want to, I drop my arm that's keeping her captive to me. I'll be patient for her. Good thing the night's still young. Her chest heaves as she drags a finger down my chest as she takes one step backward, then another. Until finally she twists around and makes her way to the bar. I watch her every step until the song changes, and I then remember why I'm here. Sadly, it's not to convince her to spend more time with me even though that's the only thing on my mind.

Pick up your copy of Flirting with the Stranger today!

If you enjoyed *Flirting with the Enemy*, I would love it if you let your friends know so they can also experience Seth's bow ties! Feel free to leave a review for *Flirting with the Enemy* on the site from which you purchased the book, Goodreads, BookBub, or your own blog. Reviews help other readers discover my books.

You can stay up-to-date on upcoming releases and sales by joining my reader group or following me on social media.
Gia Stevens' Sassy Romance Readers
Facebook
Instagram

acknowledgments

First and foremost, I want to thank everyone who picked up this book. I think I will forever be in awe that someone wants to read my stories.

I have to thank my husband. I don't know if I would have ever started writing and publishing journey without his words of encouragement. A big shout out to Brandi Zelenka. You were there for me every step of the way and I don't think I could have done this without you.

To my creative team, you pushed me to put out the best book possible and I am so thankful to have you on my side. Thank you to my editor, Brandi at My Notes in the Margin. I tend to give you a hot mess and you make it brilliant. Thank you so my beta readers Marisa Figueiredo, Jessie Bailey, Quinn Anderson, and Jenna Zelmer.

You gave me invaluable feedback to help make my manuscript sparkle. Thank you to my proofreaders Teagan Reichuber, Katy Cuthbertson, and Tonya Fender. You helped me out so much. Meghan Quinn, thank you for all your amazing advice.

Thank you Enticing Journey Book Promotions for your amazing PR work. You made everything run smoothly.

Most of all thank you to all the bloggers, bookstagrammers, and booktokers for reading and sharing your excitement for this book. It means the world to me and I can't thank you enough. And of course, thank you to all the readers for reading my words. I hope I've been able to give you a fun escape for a few hours.

See you at the next book! Stay sassy!

about the author

Gia Stevens resides in Northern Minnesota with her husband and cat. She lives for the warm, sunny days of summer and dreads the bitter cold of winter. A romantic comedy junkie at heart, she knew she wanted her own stories to encompass those same warm and fuzzy feelings.

When she's not busy writing your next book boyfriend, Gia can be found binge watching TV shows that aired five years ago, taking pictures of her cat, or curled up with a steamy romance novel.

other titles by Gia Stevens

Want to read more sassy heroines, swoony heroes, and fun and flirty romance books?

Visit Gia's website to find a complete list of all her books.

www.ingramcontent.com/pod-product-compliance
Lightning Source LLC
Chambersburg PA
CBHW070454200726
48293CB00007B/2192